STO

**DO NOT REMOVE
CARDS FROM POCKET**

The Bet's On,
Lizzie Bingman!

Rhea Beth Ross

Houghton Mifflin Company
Boston   1988

Library of Congress Cataloging-in-Publication Data

Ross, Rhea Beth.
  The bet's on, Lizzie Bingman! / Rhea Beth Ross.
    p.   cm.
  Summary: Fourteen-year-old Lizzie's bet with her oldest brother
about women's deserving equal rights kicks off a summer of
unprecedented adventure for her as she experiences things a
young lady of 1914 rarely does.
  ISBN 0-395-44472-1
  [1. Brothers and sisters — Fiction. 2. Women's rights — Fiction.
3. United States — Social conditions — 1865–1918 — Fiction.]
I. Title.
PZ7.R71983Be   1988   87-30199
[Fic] — dc19   CIP
                             AC

Printed in the United States of America

P   10 9 8 7 6 5 4 3 2 1

To Donald and Autumn and Nathan

✳ Contents ✳

❋ The Bet ❋

Most everyone in Granby remembers the summer of 1914 as when the town got electricity. I remember that hot, blustery season because it was when I gave up my dolls and jacks and lace-legged bloomers to grow up. Mother and Papa and my three brothers remember it as the time Elizabeth Bingman got what was coming to her.

I was fourteen going on fifteen. My oldest brother, Jack, was nearly seventeen. Below me in the line-up was Edman, who was thirteen going on fifty-two, and George, nine, going on three. We were all born and raised in Granby, a typical mining town tucked in the Ozark hills of southwest Missouri.

Granby had a population of three thousand, most of which worked in the lead mines or supplied products and services to the miners. Papa owned and operated the B & O Mining Company that did the smelting work for the lesser mines that surrounded the town. Papa also belonged to a civic group, the Citizen and Community Advocates, who planned the cultural entertainment for the town.

On the afternoon of June 30, the C & CA scheduled one of their sponsored events at the Lux Theater, which sat at the end of Main Street. It was an oration contest. That very event was what sparked a growing feeling in my heart that not everything was exactly fair and equal between the sexes, and set me on a crooked path in search of my rights as a woman.

My brother Jack was an entrant in the contest. He was a debater and had polished his art throughout high school. Because he was going to be a senior, he thought he had a man-sized brain. I thought he was getting too big for his britches, despite the fact that Mother had made him wear the new trousers she had ordered special delivery for him from the Sears, Roebuck catalog.

When we got to the auditorium on the afternoon of the speeches, the place was already crowded. We were late because Papa had spent most of the time since lunch polishing the bell of his tuba. He was in the Granby Miners Band, who insisted on playing at every local social function.

Before Papa took his place between the baritone and trumpet, he seated Mother and me toward the front of the theater. We always got some of the best seats in the house, those behind the mayor and the banker. Mother liked to say Papa got the special treatment because he was a respected and responsible citizen. I thought he got the seat he wanted because he weighed over two hundred pounds and had arms like oak branches and an Irish temper that flared even brighter than his flaming hair.

Edman and George plunked down beside us. Jack hurried to his place on the stage.

After a rousing chorus of "Oh! Susannah," Papa joined us at our seats and a clammy hush fell over the crowd as Jules Hilker, the master of ceremonies, stood up and made the opening statement. "Ladies and gentlemen, on behalf of the Citizen and Community Advocates, I welcome you here today to our annual declamation contest."

A lot of applause followed. Mr. Hilker leaned back on his heels, grabbed hold of one of his suspenders with his left hand, and waved his free hand at the crowd as if to tell them to control themselves so he could get on with his speech.

He continued, "We welcome you on behalf of the speakers today." He gestured toward the scraggly group of young men lined up in rows behind him on the stage.

Jack was standing in the front row of orators-to-be. I glanced at Mother and she was smiling at him, her face radiant with pride. Jack gave us a flit of a wave and began to scratch at his legs. His new suit was part wool, and I knew it was making him itch like mad. But he wouldn't have complained to Mother.

When I leaned forward in my chair to get a better look at the contestants, Mother whispered, "Lizzie, sit up straight. Please act like the lady you are." Her voice had an edge to it.

I smiled sheepishly and glanced beyond Mother to see Papa motioning for George to trade places with Edman and sit within "flipping" distance of him. George's sole reason for living, as far as I was concerned, was to make life miserable for everyone else.

Just as the mayor stepped to the stage and began his

welcoming speech, George threw a spitball at old Essie Berger who was sitting to the side of us. The paper wad hit her piled-high hair and stuck there, looking as if a low-flying bird had dropped her a present. Papa quickly leaned over and snapped George on his sleeve. He motioned for George to bend toward him. George obliged and nodded slowly as Papa whispered steadily into his ear.

I knew what the hushed lecture was about. When George got home, he was going to get it. That was Papa's way with the boys. Any broken rule was mended in the woodshed behind the house. It was punishment reserved for my brothers. Papa had never raised a hand to me, mostly because Mother believed if a young girl was treated like a lady, she would become a lady.

Mother's method of discipline was based on learning and concentration, which meant memorizing huge hunks of the Bible. I knew more scripture than any preacher we had ever had at the Methodist church. I quoted Proverbs like a second tongue and could correctly give the names of all direct kin of Adam and Eve.

Mr. Hilker tapped his gavel on the podium and announced, "Today's first speaker is Tommy Walters. His subject is 'How to Have a More Profitable Milking Operation.' "

The spectators clapped for Tommy. The old men in bibbed overalls sat up, shifted the tobacco in their cheeks, and listened to see if a sixteen-year-old hayseed could give them any advice on how to make their moon-eyed Bossies give cheese.

By the time Jack stood behind the speaker's stand, the

auditorium had begun to steam from the summer heat. The ladies were waving fans advertising Spencer's Funeral Home as if they were trying to take to flight. Most of the men were wiping their brows with giant-sized bandanas. Papa was working hard to keep the moisture from his face by mopping his beard with his handkerchief. He would stop on the upward sweeps to straighten his mustache.

I could feel big drops of water collecting between my shoulder blades. They slipped down the trough in my back and landed "splish" on my bloomers. Mother would say young ladies do not sweat — they perspire. The fat blobs of moisture on my back felt like sweat — pure old undiluted body water.

I glanced at Mother, and she signaled for me to use my fan. I began to wave the wicker monstrosity in front of my face. It made the hair on the neck of the man sitting in front of me curl and uncurl.

Mother gave me a disapproving glare, and I stopped fanning so wildly. She and I hadn't been on good terms for the last two weeks. It started when Papa's youngest sister, Esther, came from St. Louis to visit us.

Aunt Esther had hopped spryly out of the Union Pacific passenger car she had traveled in, carrying her own carpetbag and flaunting a fashionable dress that was hemmed at her mid-calves. Even before we left the depot she started telling tales about the Women's Movement that was well received in the city. To top it off, her fingernails were painted a gaudy pink color.

When Mother saw her, she gasped as if her corset had snapped. On the buggy ride home she gave Esther a lengthy lecture about the contributions an aunt should make to the proper upbringing of her niece and nephews. This was interpreted as, "You will keep all that woman's rights nonsense to yourself on this visit!"

Aunt Esther obliged my parents and said nothing about her cause in front of them, but on the sly she filled me with wonderful tales about women running for school offices, taking their places in business, and, that dream of dreams, having the right to vote in public elections.

One morning Aunt Esther let me wear her high-cut skirt to breakfast. By that afternoon, my beloved progressive aunt was back on board the Union Pacific. Supposedly, she had been called back to the city on short notice. I figured the short notice had come from Mother through Papa to Esther.

After Aunt Esther had gone, Mother sat beside me in the parlor and gave me her WOMANHOOD AND ITS DUTIES lecture. It was about the hundredth time I'd heard it. She spoke in a "proper" voice as she said, "Ladies do not go out into the sun without a parasol. Ladies do not whistle, speak loudly, run through the streets, gossip, smoke or drink, or attend vulgar shows. Ladies do sing in the church choir, play the piano, bake splendid cakes, sew with delicate skill, tend the children, and wait on the men."

When Mother wasn't watching me, I'd mouth along with her, "Men in turn provide and care for the ladies. They protect them and their reputations at all costs, and . . ."

I always wanted to add, "And treat them like overgrown children." That's the way it had always been with

Mother and me. We had Papa and the boys to shelter us from harm and disgrace, as she would put it. In my case, I wasn't always so sure I wanted them to.

I grew weary of red-haired brothers running after me and treating me like an oddity at a sideshow. On the other hand, Mother would have been at home as a porcelain-headed doll on a shelf in a carnival tent, waiting for a big, strong man to win her as the prize. Shelf-sitting was not my idea of a good time.

Despite Jack's big-headedness I felt good about the way he pleased the audience with his strong boy-man voice and his watermelon slice smile.

He began, "My topic today is Woman Suffrage." He stopped talking and let a murmur that had risen in the crowd die away.

I felt my heart fly to my throat and lodge between my tonsils. A glance at Mother told me she had helped Jack write his speech. Her face was glowing like a kid's on Christmas morning.

"There are two worlds in which we live," Jack continued formally. "The world of outside interests and the world of the home. Women belong in the home!"

There was loud applause, even from most of the women.

Jack preached, "Have there been greater rights given to women in the states that allow voting among their female inhabitants than in the states that do not? Has there been a better way of life exhibited, let's say, in the states of Wyoming and Utah?"

A cabbage-faced farmer yelled, "No, son!"

"What would happen if women were given the right to

elect officials?" There was no response. "I'll tell you what would happen," Jack promised. He leaned on the speaker's stand and eyed all of us in the front rows. "Suffrage would end chivalry. Suffrage would put undue stress on the system of the delicate, emotional female. Suffrage would divide households, turning wife against husband and increasing the divorce rate. Suffrage would cause undue suffering of little children left alone or in the care of substitute mothers while their rightful caretakers flaunted their ideals in public and paraded the streets for their rights."

Loud applause again answered his bellowing. To me, Jack sounded like a homesick calf bawling for its mama. I couldn't understand how some of the women at the lecture could agree with my brother. Harriet Street, a delicate, emotional female according to Jack, had watched five of her six children die of smallpox last year. She was clapping strongly. Pearl Akehurst, forced after the desertion of her husband to run a laundry to support three small sons, was also applauding with her spoon-face lifted upward as if she knew the angels in Heaven were approving of her clapping.

After the people settled down, Jack said, "Besides, women already run the world indirectly — rocking the cradle, teaching manners and social customs, and instructing their children in the rights and duties of American citizens."

More applause.

"Let us shelter them. Let us protect them — the best things in our lives. Let us keep them from the stresses and strains of the workaday world, the conflicts and confusion of politics, and the indecency and infractions of the courtroom. No lady should have to sit in the jury box and hear vulgar testimony and then be called upon to judge the filth that evil spawns in the world!"

I couldn't listen to any more. A line Jack had yelled had struck me in the heart like a knife. The best *things* in our lives, he had said. He had called women *things*.

I ignored the applause that followed Jack's speech. I refused to watch as he stepped forward at the end of the competition to receive the ten dollar first prize from the editor of the *Granby Gazette*. When the people began to leave, I walked unfeelingly behind Mother to the outside of the theater and climbed into the buggy. Jack had betrayed me. Mother had disowned her own sex. I felt as if a mule had kicked me in the head.

At home there was a lot of back-slapping. Relatives stopped by to congratulate Jack on his *wonderful* oratorical performance. Uncle John said from under his store-bought hair, "You'll be able to take that speech to the state competition come next September."

Jack soaked up the compliments like a sponge drawing water.

Papa was so proud of Jack that he forgot to whip George, so I even missed what would have been the highlight of my day. I sat in the front porch swing and waited listlessly for Edman to finish cranking the ice cream freezer. I wasn't even sure Mother's apricot sherbet would put any joy back into my life.

When Mother called me to help dip the ice cream and serve the cookies to Jack's following, I trudged to the kitchen. Aunt Mittie was already filling bowls with the peach-colored cream. She had lived with Mother and Papa since the summer after Jack was born. She had come to spend a vacation and ended up staying when she got word that Howard, her husband and Papa's oldest brother, had been killed in Cuba fighting at the side of Teddy Roosevelt.

Aunt Mittie didn't even go back to her home in Little Rock to get her things. A friend packed her belongings and sent them by freight to Granby. The only memory of her husband she kept alive was through a myna bird she bought at a pet store in Joplin a couple of years after Uncle Howard's death. She named the bird Santiago after the place where her husband fell in battle, but called the myna Santee for short.

Aunt Mittie was ten years Mother's senior, but she didn't really look that much older. She had a face that would stay the same until the undertaker put her down and, according to what Mother said behind her back, "a basically vulgar personality."

Aunt Mittie watched me battle the ice cream ladle for a couple of minutes, then said, "You didn't much like Brother Jack's speech."

I glanced at her and answered, "That's right."

"Your brother has some set ideas in his young mind," she said loudly, probably so Mother could hear in the pantry where she was arranging cookies on a tray.

"They're wrong ideas," I insisted.

From the pantry came Mother's raised voice, "Lizzie, I expect you to oblige your brother by at least not causing him any discomfort on this, his day!"

I looked to Aunt Mittie for help, but she only shrugged and crumbled a cookie for Santee to nibble on. The bird said, "Charge! Charge!" as it pecked at the crumbs.

Mother peeked into the kitchen, her porcelain-doll face still glowing with approval of Jack's speech. "Did you hear me, young lady?" she asked.

"Yes, ma'am," I answered reluctantly as I carried two bowls of sherbet to the back porch. I was going to find Jack and give him his treat — but good.

I found my pride-bloated brother standing by the barn, talking with Tommy Walters. I walked over to them and handed my bowl of ice cream to Tommy. "Your speech was real nice," I told him.

Tommy said, "Thank you," and walked across the yard to sit under a maple tree and eat his sherbet.

Jack reached for his bowl. I pulled it away from him.

"Give me that, Lizzie," he ordered. He tried to sound like a grown-up, but his voice cracked.

"Don't get harsh with me," I said smugly. "It might upset my delicate emotional system."

Jack shook his head and sighed as he looked across the hayfield. "I should have known you wouldn't let that speech go."

"Let it go? Brother Jack, this is the twentieth century. Women are not *things*. Men can't tell us what to do. Men can't lead us around like we're little children."

"No man wants to lead a woman around. We simply want to take care of you. We were created to take care of you."

I looked away from him.

"Besides," he added, "all that's wrong with you is that you've got a head full of Aunt Esther's stupid ideas."

"You like Aunt Esther."

"I didn't like all that hogwash she was pumping into your brain about suffering women."

"Did Mother convince you of that?" I asked.

"Don't speak badly of Mother," he warned, shaking a finger at me. "She's the greatest lady in this town. Ask anyone."

"I wasn't speaking badly of Mother —"

"Soon you will have a proper example of how a young lady should act right here in our very house," Jack said over my protest, mostly to himself.

"What do you mean?"

Again he reached for the bowl of sherbet, answering, "Cousin Hanna is coming to spend the rest of the summer with us."

My mouth fell open like a trap door.

"That's right," he continued. "Mother sent for her. She will be here before the Fourth of July."

Hanna was a year older than I was and the daughter of Mother's only living brother, but she should have been Mother's child. She reeked of sugar and spice.

"I don't need Hanna for an example of how to act. I know how to act," I insisted.

"Lizzie, Lizzie, Lizzie," Jack whispered as if he were shushing a baby. "Do you call having an egg fight with George knowing how to act? Do you call gluing Edman to the front porch swing knowing how to behave? Do you —"

"Enough!" I said quickly. "I suppose that means Edman and George don't know how to act either? I guess Mother will just have to be content with her one perfect son."

"Don't confuse the issue here, Lizzie," Jack said with his lecture voice. "Edman and George are *boys*. They have a right to be a little more foolish —"

"Who gave them that right?" I demanded.

Jack hemmed and hawed for a moment. Finally, he pronounced, "God gave them that right."

"I have read the Bible from cover to holy cover," I started. "I know most of it by heart. I don't remember any scripture that said George may throw eggs, but Lizzie shall not."

"Don't blaspheme!" Jack scolded, looking toward Heaven like a hound baying at the moon. He lowered his gaze and said, "What about Eve?"

"What about her?"

"She sinned first."

"So what?"

"She was — cursed."

"Ha!" I said hotly. "If I recall, she didn't leave the Garden of Eden alone. Seems she had a date."

"Very funny," Jack said, sneering.

"Jack, I didn't need to hear Aunt Esther's lectures to know women have rights. I've known since I was five years old and could throw a ball as far as Edman that I was just as strong as he was. I've known since I was nine and won the math fair at school that I was just as smart as any boy in my class. I've known since I was twelve and sneaked away to go hunting with you that I was just as brave as even you, big brother. I'm an equal. That's all I want — to be treated as an equal."

Jack didn't say anything.

"And you know what, Jack?"

He shook his head no.

"You used to treat me as an equal. Back when you wore knickers instead of trousers. Back when Mother had to wash behind your ears. Back when —"

"I've grown up, Lizzie," Jack said softly. "I see things more clearly now. I understand women. I know more about their needs . . ."

"Have you had this sudden burst of knowledge since you started seeing Rosie Watkins every Saturday night?"

"Rosie has got me to thinking," he admitted. "Thinking a woman does need protection. A woman does need someone strong to care for her."

"I don't," I said quickly.

"Of course you do. You don't mean that."

"I mean it. I don't need you or Edman or George to help me a bit. I don't even need Papa. I certainly don't need Mother preaching to me about it either."

"You do! You do!" Jack bellowed.

"I'll prove to you I don't," I said.

"How?"

"I'll wager you I can go the whole summer without asking for help of any kind from you or anyone else."

"If I win?"

"I'll admit women are indeed the weaker sex."

Jack scoffed, "That would be too good to be true."

"But if I win," I continued, "you have to change the

content of your speech when you take it to the state competition. You have to admit women are equal."

Jack smiled so widely his lips seemed to meet in the back of his head. "You have a deal, Lizzie girl." He leaned over and gave me a kiss on my forehead. "I sure hate to see you brought to your knees by this, but in the long run it will be worth it." He sounded like Mother with Papa's voice.

I shrugged and started toward the house.

Jack called after me, "What about my ice cream?"

I turned and walked back to him. I by-passed his outstretched hands and, with a quick pull and push, shoved the bowl of sherbet down inside his new trousers.

I walked away with a quickening pleasure in my heart. Over my shoulder I called, "Brother Jackson, the bet's on."

⁕ The Hot Seat ⁕

By the second of July, when Cousin Hanna was to arrive, Jack had succeeded in persuading George and Edman to help him in his plan to outlast me. I'm sure George was thrilled at the opportunity to keep one jump ahead of me. He liked a sporting contest and fought like a mountain lion to win.

Edman had been reluctant to join Jack's ranks at first. I could tell by the sad-eyed way he looked at me. I knew he went along with Jack mostly because Jack could whip the socks off him. At least I felt fairly certain he wouldn't carry on about the bet as much as George would.

Edman was a much quieter brother. Papa had bought him a set of encyclopedia for his eleventh birthday, and since then he had become the scholar of north Granby. He read so much that he finally needed eyeglasses. With the specs and a constant, faithful book under his arm, he looked like a professor.

When we went to the train station to meet Hanna, Papa and the boys stood on the loading platform under

the water tower to listen for the loud sounds signaling
the coming locomotive. Mother made me sit with her in
the Ladies' Waiting Room so I wouldn't get my good
dress and gloves dirty. The only amusements in there
were watching the fleas crawl on the station master's
prize blue-tick hound and reading the posters hung on
the wall — IRA SPENCER, STALLION SERVICES AVAILABLE (for
lovesick mares); QUILTING PARTY AT THE BAPTIST CHURCH ON
THE NINTH OF AUGUST (for gossip-sick mares).

I stood up when I heard the long howl of the train
whistle. Papa was nearly as noisy as the locomotive as he
shouted orders to the boys to "Stand back. Get off that
luggage rack. Tuck in your shirts."

I peered out the window and hoped the engineer
would overshoot the station platform and dump Hanna
somewhere outside of town.

Mother cleared her throat and ordered, "Lizzie, stop
gawking about like an old chicken and sit down this
minute!" She glared at me until I slipped back onto the
hard, straight-backed chair. She then added, "Please
take out your handkerchief and wipe the perspiration
from your brow."

I fumbled a handkerchief from my handbag and
dabbed at my face, under Mother's steady observation,
until the train skidded to a stop in front of the station.

Mother and I didn't stand up until Papa escorted
Hanna into the waiting room. As he brought her to us, he
gallantly removed his hat and said, "Ladies, your niece
and cousin, Hanna Gilford."

Cousin Hanna beamed like a rosebud under the dew.

Her cherry-colored cheeks framed her perfectly formed smile as she said to Mother, "Pleased to be spending the summer with you, Aunt Lana."

Mother smiled widely, letting her cornflower eyes meet Hanna's equally blue blinkers for a moment. She turned to me and asked, "Lizzie, where are your manners?"

I stammered, "Pleased to have you here, Cousin Hanna." My mouth was as dry as a cotton bale on a tin roof.

Hanna smiled one of her six-cornered smiles and began to chat with Mother about the trip, the heat, the folks at home. You name it, they talked about it. Softly, of course. Privately, of course. That was the difference in visiting and gossiping, according to Mother. What I heard sounded like tall tales, but then I didn't say that.

When I walked outside I saw the boys were loading what looked like a dozen trunks into the freight wagon Jack had driven to town to haul Hanna's luggage back to the farm. They ignored me until I tried to unfasten my parasol. It was stuck at the clasp.

Edman leaned over the wagon to help me, but Jack slipped a firm hand on his shoulder and told him to arrange the trunks a little closer to the front of the wagon.

I glared at Jack and managed to snap open the parasol in time for a strong, southerly breeze to turn it inside out and pop the pink yarn ball off its top. The decoration blew across the street and landed at the door of Henderson's Mercantile.

I got so mad, I threw the whole contraption into a

water trough by the station just in time for Mother to walk out onto the platform with Hanna Dear and see my tantrum. She only gave me a sideways glance and said sternly, "That will be the first five chapters of Psalms for you, young lady,"as she took hold of Papa's outstretched hand and let him seat her beside Hanna in the buggy.

I leaned against the wagon for a moment, watching Jack watch me out of the corner of his eye. I said to myself, "Blessed is the man that walketh not in the counsel of the ungodly, nor standeth in the way of sinners, nor sitteth in the seat of the scornful . . ." It promised to be a long, Biblical summer.

The morning of the Fourth of July everyone at home got up early to finish chores before we headed to town for the celebration. The boys were well into their summer business enterprises. Jack had a melon patch. It covered about two and a half acres, and he had planted it with Hearts of Gold and Rocky Fords, hoping, of course, to make a killing selling slices of melon to the people attending the autumn harvest festival.

Edman and George had set themselves up in the hen-and-chick business. The first day of July they had gone down to the mercantile and bought five settings of fertile eggs from Mrs. Henderson. They had taken their brown-shelled wonders out to the coal shed and stuffed them under five broody hens. Anticipating peeping chicks in about three weeks and money in their pockets in about eight, they pestered the old hens endlessly to be certain they were doing their duties.

Papa finally had to round up his "businessmen" so we could start for town. It was after seven, and the road was already full of wagons and buggies headed toward the picnic grounds.

Mother was dressed in a cream-colored shift. Hanna wore a dress identical to it, except for the addition of a bright yellow ribbon tied at her waist. Aunt Mittie decided to be practical and wore a gray twill frock; she thought wearing something frilly to a picnic was the stupidest stunt a woman could pull.

Mother ignored Aunt Mittie's suggestions about comfort, and instead dressed us kids according to style. She had made the boys striped britches to wear to the festivities and had purchased three short-sleeved tan silk shirts to complete their outfits.

Mother had made me a white gown to wear in the pageant that afternoon. It had a strip of red, white, and blue bunting that was to run from my left shoulder to my right hip for the play. She said I couldn't wear the sash until we got to town, despite my begging. When I wouldn't stop bothering her about it, she assigned me another three chapters in Psalms.

At seven-thirty we headed up Main Street to the center of activity. I was packed in beside George and the iced washtub full of potato salad, thick cream, and lemonade. Edman sat across from us with a book called *Gulliver's Travels*. When he read, his lips moved and made a swishing sound. He stopped his study only once when Mother ordered him to cover the basket of fried chicken before the flies carried it away.

Papa and Jack parked the buggy and wagon beside the

hardware store and unhitched the teams. Jack tied the horses to a tether line while Papa called us to him. He dug deep into the inside pocket of his jacket and pulled out his soft leather wallet.

Jack walked over to him and took the three dollar bills Papa passed his way. With undue reverence Edman received two dollars. And George stood patiently waiting for his dollar.

They sauntered away after they had received their allowances. Jack had pocketed his money. Edman had used his as a bookmark. And George was fondling his cash with his grubby little hands as if he had been given the key to the city.

I knew I was about to get another dose of inequality when Papa put away his wallet and pulled out his coin purse. He handed me a half dollar with great ceremony as he said, "For my darling daughter."

I considered saying, "No thank you, Generous One," but Papa's mustache was twitching at a rapid rate, so I held out my palm and took the gift. I knew Papa thought he was being entirely fair. After all, a young lady wouldn't need money to do all the things the boys would do. Like take her turn at the target-shooting booth, or pay someone to guess her weight, or buy a ticket to see the boa-constrictor-brought-from-South-America-by-a-tattooed-man-who-sweated-ink. In fact, none of the fun things.

After Papa retrieved his tuba from the wagon and strutted toward the grandstand to join the other members of the Miners Band for rehearsal before their afternoon concert, I resigned myself to a day of boredom and followed Mother, Aunt Mittie, and Hanna the Magnificent to Picnic Hill. The boys tagged along behind us, lugging the heavy baskets and tubs full of our lunch.

Mother smiled and waved at her friends as we weaved through the crowd to find a place to sit in the shady grove that overlooked Granby. Picnic Hill was one of the prettiest places in the countryside. It was so much higher than the rest of the town that the smoke from the smelter didn't wilt the foliage on it. Papa reluctantly admitted that fumes and ash from the lead processor could be the death of us all, with it puking its gray filth all over the stores and streets and houses.

The only time Mother worried about the soot was on Monday, washday. If you wanted to hear her at her worst, it would be on a sunny, laundry-day morning when the fresh clothes were hanging on the line and the wind would shift, sending black smoke in and out of the dropseat in Papa's drawers.

Mother finally found a secluded spot under an oak tree and told Jack to spread the quilts on the ground for her. Jack obliged, even going so far as to sweep the grass for acorns before he smoothed the blankets in the shade. He gave Mama, Aunt Mittie, and Hanna a hand down to their seats. He looked hatefully at me. To make him mad I plopped down, crossed my legs Indian style, and put my elbows on my knees.

Jack turned away quickly, and Mother scolded, "Lizzie, stop that!"

I watched Mother and Hanna unpack the food, until Hanna accidentally stuck her long, delicate fingers into the tray of deviled eggs and cried shrilly, "I've dirtied my hand! May I please have a napkin?"

Smiling at her like a sick calf, Mother said, "Of course, dear. Here you are," as she handed Hanna a gingham cloth.

I felt my stomach somersault, so I asked to be excused.

Mother raised her eyebrows and said, "I don't think it's a very good idea for you to be gallivanting about the streets alone, Lizzie. Get one of your brothers to go with you."

I would rather have eaten lizards and toads.

Aunt Mittie popped up and said, "I'll go with you to see the sights, Lizzie." I could have kissed her smack on the lips.

"I guess that would be all right." Mother surrendered.

I stood still while Aunt Mittie helped me tie the red, white, and blue sash to my dress. "You look very nice," she said as she stepped back to take a longer look at me.

Hanna sighed loudly.

Mother sat up and said proudly, "Mittie is right, you do look beautiful, daughter." Then she reached into her handbag and pulled out a dollar. "Here's a little something for you to spend."

Mother wasn't looking right at me. She was glancing from side to side as if she was watching a fly flit on the porch screen.

"Papa gave me some money," I told her.

"Was it enough?" Mama asked quickly. But before I could answer, she said, "Of course, it was enough. Your papa takes fine care of us all." Then she crammed the money back into her bag and smiled at Hanna.

Aunt Mittie took me by the arm and half-dragged me down the hill. Behind us, Mother called out, "Lizzie, lunch is precisely at noon."

I waved that I had heard.

When we were out of earshot, Aunt Mittie said, "Your mother is going to proper herself to death. It's that fancy New Orleans upbringing of hers. Practically ruined her in my opinion. It'll be a hot day in January when that woman gets some sense about living."

Aunt Mittie walked with me across the watered-down and oiled main street. Besides trying to keep the dust under control, the Citizen and Community Advocates had also provided huge tanks filled with iced water, and benches made with hunks of stove wood and planks from the lumberyard. The town looked really nice.

In front of the barber shop, Aunt Mittie met Clinton Thompson, her unofficial beau. Mother disapproved of him so much that Aunt Mittie dreaded bringing him to the house. So they courted mostly at church socials and picnics. I liked Mr. Thompson. He smelled of a strange combination of kerosene and bay rum cologne. Mother said it was pure alcohol I was smelling, but I liked it anyway.

The two lovebirds strolled away from me. Aunt Mittie called over her shoulder, "Remember, Lizzie, lunch is at noon. I don't want your mother after both of us."

After another fifteen minutes of wandering through the streets, I had given up finding any entertainment and was about to rejoin the blanket brigade on Picnic Hill when I heard a friendly, familiar voice call to me, "Hey, Lizzie, what you doing?"

I turned around to see Teddy Hargrove, my usual ally in crime, walking toward me. Teddy and I had been suspended from school for a day this past year for rigging the teacher's chair to tip over when he took his imperial seat. Jack and Edman hated Teddy because they said he always cheated playing games and swore like a sailor, though I had never seen him act like a bad sport or heard a foul word come out of his mouth. And last summer Teddy had held George under water at the swimming hole until he bubbled. That made all three of my brothers his for-life enemies.

I turned to Teddy and answered, "I'm not doing much, Mr. Hargrove. Fighting boredom."

He grinned like a Cheshire cat and asked, "Would a ride on the merry-go-round suit you?"

"Papa only gave me a half dollar," I said. "And I was planning on buying some orange pop and floss candy."

Teddy smiled again and said, "My treat." He pulled a yard-long streamer of tickets out of his pants pocket.

"Where did you get those?" I asked in amazement.

"I've got a job at the dunking booth when they open it this afternoon," he answered promptly. "I'm on the hot seat."

"What is a hot seat?"

"Tell you what. After our ride I'll take you over there and let you see where I'll be working." He took hold of my elbow and escorted me to the merry-go-round. The steam engine ground to a halt and a circle of riders scrambled off the wooden horses. Teddy helped me aboard a blazing blue stallion. He took the mount to my right — a bright red steed with flaring nostrils. We laughed and sang as the stampeding herd made turn after turn above the sawdust.

When the ride was over, Teddy bought me a sack of peanuts and the pop I had wanted. We strolled up the main boulevard. I walked as close to Teddy's side as I dared to get. I wasn't old enough to court yet, and I wasn't quite sure what my brothers would do if they caught me in the company of their declared enemy number one.

Teddy whispered into my ear, "You sure look pretty today, Lizzie. Dressed in white like that — like a fairy princess."

I felt my cheeks color as I mumbled, "The dress is for the pageant this afternoon. I'm Miss Liberty."

"Quite an honor. Quite an honor," Teddy marveled, stepping to my side to take a longer look at my outfit. "You're the prettiest Miss Liberty we've ever had."

I blushed again. I knew the only reason I had been chosen for the coveted role of Miss Liberty was because Mother was on the pageant planning committee. She had argued that the heroine of the play could indeed have freckles and auburn hair and be as lovely as the usual clear-skinned and cotton-topped girls who had played the part for the sixty-four years of the town's tradition.

I was still glowing at Teddy's compliments when I saw

a hand grab him on the shoulder from behind and whirl him around. Edman stood there, a look of defiance magnified in his spectacles. "What are you doing with my sister, Hargrove?"

Teddy smiled like a kid caught with his hand in the cookie jar. "Just showing her the sights," he answered wisely.

"I'll show her the sights," Edman said firmly as he stepped between Teddy and me.

"I don't want you to show me the sights," I told Edman. I almost wished I had kept my mouth shut when I saw his face fall like a rock in the well.

"What's he got that I don't have?" Edman demanded, sounding hurt.

"You're my brother. Besides, Teddy bought me a drink and a ride on the merry-go-round."

"I have money. I'll buy you things," Edman protested.

"It's not the same," I said as I stepped to Teddy's side.

Teddy looked into my face and said, "Come on, Lizzie. I'll win you a Kewpie doll."

"It's my duty as her brother to win her the doll," Edman said. He pulled me away from my escort.

Teddy bristled like a cat and for a moment he and Edman stared pointblank into each other's eyes. Finally, Teddy challenged, "At the shooting booth. Five minutes. Put your money where your mouth is, Bingman."

"All right, best shot wins," Edman agreed loudly.

I followed Teddy through the crowd to the booth

where a man ran a contest using twenty-two-caliber rifles to hit a small target set up on a tree about thirty feet from the leaning counter.

The match was one-sided the moment Edman picked up a rifle and managed to miss the target on his first three shots. After that I knew he didn't have as much chance as a grasshopper in a hen yard. Teddy held the gun against his shoulder and with a smug look squeezed six rounds into the bull's eye.

Teddy not only won me a Kewpie doll, he also managed to clean house with Edman's pocket money. Edman acknowledged his loss and coughed up his last nickel in a weak effort to hit the target for the last time. He missed and hit a tin cup six feet from the shooting booth.

I felt sort of sorry for Edman. I watched him mope across the street like a whipped puppy to talk to Jack. But I managed to give both brothers a defiant smile as I let Teddy lead me toward the dunking booth where he would reign supreme that afternoon.

Teddy was proud of his job. He puffed up like a toad when he explained to me that every boy in town had tried to get the privilege of sitting on the hot seat. He said even Jack had signed up for it. I knew Teddy's outdoing Jack had probably caused Jack to rate him even lower than a dog's belly.

The dunking booth was an odd contraption set up with a bull's eye out to one side and a seat perched over a tank of water on the other. The object of the game was to buy three balls for a nickel, throw them at the bull's eye, and when the target was hit, it would trigger a spring which would lower the seat the "dunkee" was on, and he would fall into the tank.

Teddy climbed onto the seat and said, "The view from here is great. I can see all the way down the street. Want to take a look?"

I glanced toward the sidewalk and answered, "Oh, maybe I shouldn't."

"Come on, it's safe." He climbed down and held out a hand to me. "All the balls are stored. No one can dunk you."

I smiled as I let Teddy seat me on the hot seat. He was right, the view was great. I could see everything. Everything, like my brother George coming toward the booth with an evil look in his eye. Everything, like the two-pound boulder George had had in his hand whirling through the air. And everything, like the target tipping back, the spring popping, and me in my red, white, and blue sashed dress dropping into the filled tank.

I hit the water with a thud and sank to the bottom, dusting my backside on the moss-covered tank. By the time I got air, George was gone. I knew he was probably behind some concession stand, lemonade in hand, laughing his evil little heart out.

Teddy pulled me from the mire and tried the best he could to wipe the water off my clothing. The patriotic-colored bunting made my white dress look like a rainbow as it ran and spread Old Glory across my chest, down my skirt, probably through to my camisole and bloomers.

"I'm so sorry," Teddy kept repeating like a parrot.

"It's all right. There was nothing you could have done about it," I moaned.

He breathed deeply. "What are your folks going to say?"

"I don't even want to think about it."

I gave him a tiny wave as I made my way through the back streets to Picnic Hill. When Mother saw me, her eyes snapped flame like a firecracker. She didn't speak to me during my entire explanation, but after I had finished my defense, she stood up and walked over to where Reverend Pike was having his lunch.

In a few minutes she returned, carrying the good preacher's Bible. She said flatly, "Psalms, chapters nine through twenty." She handed me The Book.

I untied the bunting from around my waist and gave it to her, sat down, opened the scriptures to the Book of Songs, and began to memorize.

Jack joined us a few minutes later. He was holding something behind his back. He took a look at me, a look at the soaked bunting, and a look at Mother's face drawn into a wrinkled red and black wad, like an embarrassed walnut shell. "What happened to Lizzie?" he demanded.

"Teddy Hargrove was at the root of it," Mother answered.

I started to protest, because she hadn't even mentioned what George had done, but Mother clicked at me, sounding like a cricket.

"That right, Lizzie?" Jack asked, giving me his brother-knows-best look.

I didn't answer him.

He pulled his hidden hand from behind his back and

threw a Kewpie doll at me. He said sarcastically, "For my dear sister who means so much to me." He stamped down the hill.

There wasn't much consolation in knowing Brother Edman won the watermelon-eating contest (which would mean endless trips to the outhouse), or that Mother's chocolate cake won first prize at the dessert fair, or that the Thearle-Duffield Company — the best in the explosives business — was in charge of the fireworks spectacular at dark, or that George would surely take a trip with Papa to the woodshed when we got home.

There wasn't much consolation at all for being grounded to a blanket for the entire Fourth of July celebration, Bible in lap, or in knowing that my cousin, Miss Proper Priss, was going to play my part in the pageant.

Even after I dried off and had a sandwich I still felt bad. I felt worse when I saw Jack and Edman march triumphantly up the hill to watch the fireworks display.

They sat down beside me on the blanket. Their smirking faces were nearly glowing in the dark.

"Why are you boys so happy?" Mother asked suspiciously.

"No reason," Jack said.

George ran up the hill after them and slid to a stop beside the leftover chocolate cake. "You should have seen them, Mother," he cried.

"Whatever are you talking about?" she asked.

"Jack and Edman dunked that old Teddy Hargrove all afternoon. They hit the target near every time. Teddy even wanted to quit, but the man who hired him made him stay because he had spent nearly all his pay," George explained breathlessly.

"Where did you boys get money to do that?" Mother asked Jack.

"Sold our pocket knives," he answered flatly.

Mother nodded and looked at me as she said, "See what you forced your brothers to do, Lizzie? Sometimes, I think you are undeserving of your family. I'll take the dolls that were won for you. You need no souvenir of such a day as this one."

I picked up the Kewpie doll Teddy had won for me and the one Jack had dumped in my lap and handed them to Mother. As I watched my brothers enjoying their victory over me, I envied their freedom. I felt sorry for myself. Sorry enough to turn down ice cream. Sorry enough not to applaud for the fireworks. The only one I figured was sorrier than me was poor Teddy. I figured he looked like a prune.

* The Burial *

For the whole week after the Fourth of July, Papa was so "tooted out" from playing his tuba at the band concert that all he did was sit on the front porch or walk back and forth to the smelter. He developed a deep rumbling cough on Wednesday but said he was going to put in a whole day's work anyway.

Mother was not very happy about him going off to work sick. She made him wear a poultice around his neck. It smelled like kerosene. I saw him pitch it under the lilac bush by the front gate when he left the house.

At noon, Mother had me take Papa his lunch pail. Of course, she thought I should be accompanied by a brother. Edman was selected. He seemed fairly agreeable about it and read *Gulliver's Travels* while we walked along.

Truth of it was I didn't mind having Edman along. I didn't like the smelter. It frightened me. It seemed to be a giant with a big, gray mouth that pulled in and chomped up bits of the shiny lead and silicate the miners fed to it. The noise was deafening, often sounding like a woman screaming or wolves at hunt. I walked quickly and hoped Edman wouldn't suspect I was afraid.

Edman stayed in the yard while I went into the smelter to find Papa. He was sitting beside the furnace in the main room. Eager for his meal, he motioned for me to hurry.

I opened his lunch pail and took the container of coffee off the top so he could heat it on the metal oven. He reached inside the bucket and set out his deviled eggs and ham sandwiches, spreading a checkered cloth over his knees as he started to eat.

"Thank you, Lizzie girl," he said through a breaded bite. He dug inside his shirt pocket for the customary dime he gave to the child who brought him his lunch.

I kissed Papa on the cheek as I took the money, and left to find Edman, who was sitting beside a pile of coal with his nose stuck in his book. As I walked past him he said, "Half that dime is mine."

"That's what you think. All you did was stumble along behind me, kicking dust on my stockings."

"Half mine," he insisted. He pulled himself up, dog-eared his page, and tucked his book under his arm. "I protected you on your journey here."

"That wasn't my idea. I didn't ask for your help."

Edman looked over the top of his glasses. "Who are you trying to fool, Lizzie? All us boys know you're scared of walking to the smelter by yourself."

"I am not," I said. "Besides, you didn't offer much protection anyway. What if a murderer had been lying along the road, waiting in ambush to jump on me?"

Edman shrugged.

"He would've had to have killed me with your book for you even to have noticed."

Edman stood silent for a moment. Then a slow smile crept across his face. "I'll tell Jack."

"Tell him what?"

"That you didn't treat me as an equal."

"That has nothing to do with the bet."

"Seems if you want to be an equal, we boys should be equal to you, too. So, fair and square, you owe me a nickel."

"I won't pay. And you can tell Jack anything you please. I don't need any of my lily-livered, yellow-bellied brothers walking along to protect me without my consent, then asking me to pay for it."

Edman's spectacles slid to the very tip of his nose and his mouth opened like a gaping trench. "Lily-livered? Yellow-bellied? We'll see what Jack has to say about that."

"Why don't you leave Jack out of this? Be your own man, Edman Bingman!"

Edman turned and stared at me, looking crushed. He tried to speak, but nothing came out. He gasped like a banked fish. With a defiant shake of his head he ran away.

When I got to the stretch of road beside the house I saw Jack. He swaggered toward me, as if he held the wisdom of the world. As he stood in front of me he said in a very manlike voice, "So, your brothers are cowards and you don't need their protection?"

Instead of answering him, I stepped around him and started toward home.

Jack threw himself in front of me, his hand out-stretched. "Edman said you didn't give him his share of the dime."

"Good grief! What was I supposed to do, bite it in half?"

Jack reached out and caught my right fist, dime enclosed.

"Let go of me."

"The dime," he demanded. His eyes were a dirty-brown color, like mud on the creek bank.

"All right." I wiggled my arm so he would loosen his hold on my wrist. When he set me free, I dropped the coin inside my blouse.

"Elizabeth Bingman, get that out of there!"

"If you want it so badly, you get it, Brother Jack."

He growled like a bear and slapped his hand on his thigh. "Dang you, I'm going to tell Mother."

"If I were Rosie, you would go after that dime in a minute."

Jack made his hands into fists and pounded the air. "You make me so mad, Lizzie. I ought to . . ."

"Go ahead, punch me one in the nose. I'm all for equality," I dared.

Edman ran over to us. "Get my money?" he asked Jack.

Edman was sure surprised when Jack caught him around his neck and dragged him toward the house.

When I got to the house I saw a delivery wagon parked beside the back door. Mother was on the porch talking with Alta Hopkins, the butter-and-egg lady.

Mrs. Hopkins's husband, Gerald, was an invalid. He had been injured in the war with Spain. He had taken a bullet in his thigh and couldn't do a lick of work. Some people believed he didn't work because he didn't want to.

The Hopkinses' farm was passed down to them by Gerald's daddy. Everyone called the place The Goat Ranch. Its yard was full of crates and tin cans and kindling wood. The house itself was falling in on one side, and the roof buckled up on the other.

Despite what the townsfolk thought about Gerald Hopkins, no one could say his wife was lazy. She managed to keep their farm going and raise a brood of kids despite her handicaps.

Usually all the Hopkins kids tagged along with their mother on deliveries, except for the older boys, Ralph and Thomas. They worked at one of the mines to put clothing on the other eight kids' backs. For some reason, though, this time Ralph was with his mama, but the little children were nowhere in sight.

I walked over to Mother to help her carry the milk and eggs into the house. Mrs. Hopkins was known for having the finest eggs in the county. They were always fresh and usually unfertilized. I guessed with all those kids around, they had plenty of hands to slap the rooster.

I set the milk jars in the icebox on the back porch and began to put the eggs from the crate into a basket. Hanna came outside and stood beside me. She bent over and whispered, "Does Aunt Lana always buy her farm staples from this woman?"

I nodded that she did.

Hanna stood up and glared at Mrs. Hopkins. She bent down again and said, "But she's so . . . unkempt."

Hanna was right about Mrs. Hopkins being "unkempt." That was really a polite word for dirty. Funny thing about Alta Hopkins was that although she ran her business with efficiency, she was a sight.

I watched her bend over her cart and pull out a hunk of goat cheese in an attempt to sell Mother one more item. Her ragged dress was pinned at the shoulders; her large, overrun boots seemed to be holding onto her feet; and her graying hair was tucked under a holey handkerchief tied in a knot at the back of her neck.

Mrs. Hopkins drawled faintly, "Sure fine cheese, Mrs. Bingman. Smooth and fine."

Mother had decided to make the extra purchase. I could tell by the way she folded her arms across her stomach and looked directly into Mrs. Hopkins's eyes, preparing to bargain the price. It didn't surprise me that Mother bought just one thing more from the frazzled lady. Mother was that way about helping people. She kept her "regular rounds" as she called them every week, visiting the sick and the shut-in, and, as Aunt Mittie explained, "the just plain filthy and poor."

After Mother paid Mrs. Hopkins for the purchases, Hanna carried the eggs inside the house and returned to stand beside me. From the way Hanna sniffed the air, I could tell she was making sure she was upwind from Mrs. Hopkins and her essence of goat.

Suddenly, Mrs. Hopkins began to cough violently.

"You all right, Alta?" Mother asked slowly as she reached out to steady the woman.

Ralph Hopkins rushed to his mama and caught her around the waist as she nearly swooned.

"You come inside and have a nice cup of tea," Mother said to Mrs. Hopkins as she motioned for Ralph to bring his mama into the house.

Hanna flashed me a questioning look and sneered, probably at the thought of Mrs. Hopkins sitting at the kitchen table and having refreshments.

I followed Mother and her guests into the house.

"Lizzie, put on the water," Mother ordered as she and Aunt Mittie made Mrs. Hopkins comfortable.

I set the teapot on the stove and began to set out the tiny-flowered china reserved for company. Hanna flew over to me and said in a muffled voice, "Not the *good* dishes. The everyday ones will do."

"But they're *company*," I protested, only to be over-ruled as Hanna quickly set the best dishes back inside the hutch and pulled out the oatmeal-colored ones we always used.

Mother called for me to serve, so I gathered the dishes and placed them on the cabinet beside the stove. I poured the tea and carried the cup-topped saucers to the table. When I set the drinks in front of Mother, she gave me a chilling look that the Grim Reaper would have been proud to have imitated. I excused myself and joined Hanna in the parlor to finish my daily quota of embroidering.

In about thirty minutes, I heard the sound of pony bells and knew the Hopkinses were back on their rounds. As soon as the ringing faded, Mother stormed into the parlor, carrying our giant-sized family Bible.

She looked down at me like a hawk sizing up a rabbit. "Elizabeth Lee Bingman, I am so ashamed of you."

I probably looked as dumb as I felt.

Mother continued. "Alta Hopkins is no fool. She knew you served her on everyday plates."

I started to say something, but Mother shushed me.

"And to think that you, blessed with all the material wealth of this family, would turn up your nose at a woman who works as hard as Mrs. Hopkins does. Her husband a cripple; her children all working, not getting the educations they need to do better; her health poor . . ." Mother stopped for a minute and wiped away a tear that was trailing down her cheek.

I glanced across the room at Hanna. She was busily embroidering, not bothering to open her mouth and tell the truth.

I was caught between a rock and a hard place. If I told on Hanna, Mother would label me a tattletale. If I didn't tell on her, I'd have to bear the shame of being a selfish, uncaring brat. The lecture for the latter seemed to be half over, so I kept my mouth shut until Mother had finished talking, then I said solemnly, "Sorry, ma'am."

Mother gave me a searing look and opened the Bible. She handed it to me with her fingers thumping a certain passage with what could only be called righteous indignation. "Read this," she said.

I read from the Beatitudes with undeserved repentance in my heart. "Blessed are the poor in spirit: for theirs is the kingdom of heaven. Blessed are they that mourn: for they shall be comforted. Blessed are the meek: for they shall inherit the earth."

Hanna breathed deeply as I read. I hoped she would miss a stitch.

*   *   *

The next morning a neighbor came to the back door during breakfast. He talked to Papa for a few minutes outside on the porch. When he left, Papa returned to the table and announced reverently that Alta Hopkins had died in her sleep the night before.

Papa said, "Died peaceful in slumber with all her little children around her. Said the older boys didn't even know she was gone until they came back from doing their morning chores and didn't smell bacon frying."

Mother began to hurriedly clear the table. She said, "There's much to be done. Arrangements to make at the church. There's the dinner to prepare. And poor Alta," she stopped and sighed, "never had a decent dress." Mother turned to Aunt Mittie and said, "Will you please go up to my trunk and get that blue-patterned shift? It would look nice on her."

"Poor Alta worked herself to death," Papa started.

Mother interrupted with, "You know she didn't work herself to death! If hard work killed a being, most all of Granby would be dead. Consumption killed her. And if we had a clinic right here in town, there's a good chance Alta would be making her butter-and-egg rounds come tomorrow morning."

Papa sighed. "Now, Lana Lee, I tried to get the C & CA to use the extra community money to start a clinic. You know I did."

"And instead they voted to put in . . . electricity. As if the light God provided was not enough," Mother ranted. "As is, we're going to be able to see more clearly exactly who is dying."

"Putting in electricity is progress," Papa defended.

Mother didn't give up. "There's progress and there's PROGRESS. Saving and prolonging lives is true progress. Being able to see the spider webs hanging in the corners of your living room even at midnight is *not* the kind of progress *I* dream about." With that said she stormed out of the room.

Papa cleared his throat and took a long look at us kids. "Your mother is simply upset because of Mrs. Hopkins's death." When no one said anything he added, "Let's get around and about and do our chores."

Mother came back into the kitchen while Hanna and I were helping Aunt Mittie wash the dishes. She said, "Mittie, I'm going to take the dress and some undergarments over to Spencer's, then stop and make arrangements for Lily Crabtree to plan the dinner."

Spencer Lumberyard and Funeral Home was the only undertaking establishment in town. When a woman died, it was custom for another woman to be present during the embalming. Mr. Spencer didn't want to take a chance on being considered immoral or improper. More than once, Mother had been the only woman who volunteered to stay in the room during the preparation of the body. For some reason she felt it was her duty to see that every person who died in Granby had a proper burial.

As Mother gathered the clothing to take to the funeral parlor and gave Aunt Mittie last minute instructions about lunch, she handed me my bonnet. "You'll come with me, Lizzie," she said plainly as she hurried to the front door.

I put on my hat and glanced over my shoulder at Hanna. She was suddenly very busy helping Aunt Mittie. As I followed Mother out to the buggy Edman was preparing to drive for her, I got a sinking feeling in my stomach that Mother was about to teach me an unforgettable and undeserved lesson in living.

Mr. Spencer met us at the door of his business and said, "Mrs. Bingman, I was hoping you would come. They just brought Alta in, and, well, you know what they gave me to dress her in."

Mother handed Mr. Spencer the clothing she had packed and watched as he smiled warmly and touched the dress. "This will look lovely on her," he said as he turned toward the back of the store.

I was content just looking around, examining the long bundles of rope that were hanging from the ceiling beams, and soaking up the bittersweet smells of kerosene and freshly cut lumber. But Mother got my attention with a clap of her hands and motioned for me to follow her after the undertaker.

She led me to a little room behind the back counter of the store. When I walked inside and sat down on a stool, the clammy air in the place swooshed over me and made the little hairs on the back of my neck stand at attention.

Quickly removing her gloves and bonnet, Mother joined Mr. Spencer at a table on the far side of the room. I didn't dare look in that direction but, instead, stared out the only window in the place. I tried not to smell anything, or to listen to them talk, or look beyond the small patch of alley I could see through the yellowed pane. Only when we were back outside and sitting in the buggy did I breathe deeply.

I wanted to lay my head in Mother's lap and have a good cry, but I stayed stiff-backed thinking about Hanna at home, probably sitting with Aunt Mittie in the parlor, sipping lemonade, doing her beautiful embroidery, and not caring a thing about the poor or the dead or her shamed cousin taking the blame for *her* selfishness.

I felt like a martyr — a brave Christian standing in an arena surrounded by taunting Romans, hearing them shout, "Let in the lions!" I must have been smiling at my imaginary courage because Mother took a long look at me and roared, "Lizzie, this is no time to be happy!"

They laid out Alta Hopkins at her home right after noon. Mother and the other ladies from the church took covered-dish casseroles and fried chicken and freshly baked pies to the Hopkins house. Since there were no out-of-town relatives to send for, the service was to be later in the day, and burial would be before sunset.

Papa went to town to arrange for the miners to ready the grave. He said he would be home about two o'clock and told the boys they could go swimming if they would be back before supper.

I took my sewing basket to the front porch and watched the boys swagger toward Shoal Creek with their red hair on fire under the sun, their tanned arms swinging, and their long grasshopper legs taking giant strides.

It wasn't fair. Before I could swim I had to wait for Papa to come along with me. Then I had to wear a bathing suit that would weigh down a mule. The boys swam natural, not wearing a stitch of clothing. They swam in a private place upstream from where Papa let me paddle and splash. There seemed to be no justice in the world.

I was still pouting when Betsy Davis and Dorothy Cambridge came strolling down our lane. They were wearing their bathing suits covered by sleeveless dresses. Their hair was tucked under bandana handkerchiefs. "Hi, Lizzie," they called. "Come swim with us."

I almost answered that I couldn't, but I remembered that Papa was on his way to the smelter and that Mother was at the Hopkinses' where she would probably stay until almost funeral time. Aunt Mittie was taking a nap, and the boys were safely swimming upstream.

"Sure," I answered. I laid my sewing aside and hurried into the house to put on my bathing suit. I ran smack into Hanna Hateful.

"What are you doing?" she demanded.

"Going swimming." I pushed by her and took the stairs in twos.

When I got back to the door, she said, "I'm coming with you."

"Water's cold."

"If you go, I go. Or I'll tell on you."

I couldn't believe she had already forgotten I was the one who had something to tell on her. But then Mother would probably say I shouldn't have listened to Hanna about the dishes in the first place — that I should have "known better." "All right, get your clothes changed," I agreed reluctantly.

While Hanna put on her suit, I tried to explain to Betsy and Dorothy that Hanna was a bit hard to take. After the long walk to the creek, they didn't need any further convincing. Hanna griped the entire trip. *Too many rocks. Too hot. Too far to walk. She had forgotten her hairpins.*

At the creek, we all slipped into the bubbling water and cooled off. Back on shore we started our regular gossip routine about who had done what, whose brother had got it and for what, and what social events were coming up. I casually mentioned that Aunt Esther had written me a week before and sent me one of her suffrage magazines published in New York.

Betsy and Dorothy were impressed. Hanna made a humph sound.

"Aunt Esther said we should start a suffragette club in Granby," I explained.

"My pa would spank me for being a member," Betsy said shrilly.

Dorothy nodded in agreement.

"We could do it secretly," I suggested, remembering all the organizational tactics described in the magazine. "Don't you think women should have equal rights?"

Both girls nodded a slow yes. Hanna cleared her throat.

"Then we'll start the club right now, with four members," I said quickly.

Hanna said, "Not me," and stood up to leave.

"It might be fun," Betsy volunteered. "After all, it's only girls *talking* about things, nothing drastic."

Hanna sat back down and asked, "Want to be just like the boys, Lizzie?"

She had on an artificial smile I didn't trust, but I went ahead and asked, "What do you mean?"

"Prove you're equal to the boys," she teased.

"How?" I asked, afraid of what Hanna might be able to suggest under pressure.

"Prove to us you're an equal by swimming over to the boys and diving off that big rock they use."

"I'd drown in this," I said, pulling at the top of my bathing suit.

"Then swim without it," Hanna said slyly.

"In my underwear?" I asked, hardly believing that Hanna had suggested anything that daring.

Her look was smug.

Betsy and Dorothy stared at me, their eyes begging me to give it a try and put Hanna in her place.

To Hanna's open-mouthed surprise, I stood up and peeled away my bathing suit until I was dressed in only my bloomers and camisole.

"Think you can swim that far, Lizzie?" Betsy asked as I eased into the water.

I answered a bubbly, "Yes," as I paddled into the deep, toward the rock and my naked, sunning brothers.

George was the first one to see me coming. He was standing on the diving rock, bare in all his male glory, when he began to stutter and stammer something that sounded like, "Cover your privates, it's Lizzie!"

Jack rolled lazily from his back toward me, then quickly fell into the water. He stayed under for at least two minutes. All the boys diving off the rock reminded me of turtles sliding off logs into the pond.

I climbed to the diving position, and to the garbled protests of my brothers, made a floppy jump into the deep. Jack met me in the water when I surfaced and grabbed my hair. "You've done it this time, Lizzie," he said as he dunked me and held me under until I felt I had moss on the brain.

When I came up I spit a fountain of water right on top of his head.

He pushed me away, and I think I heard him curse. He swam toward the shore and his clothes with big sweeping strokes, leaving me with the other retreating brothers and a long swim back to the girls. When I climbed up the creek bank, out of breath and slightly sunburned, I saw that Hanna was gone.

"You're going to get it when you get home," Betsy announced as I pulled on my bathing suit.

"It was worth it," I said gladly, knowing I had outdone Hanna *and* my brothers.

By the time I got home and saw Mother waiting for me on the front porch with Hanna standing beside her, the declaration of "worth it" had slipped a notch of importance.

When I was within hearing distance, Mother questioned, "Elizabeth, did you undress to your undergarments and swim to where your brothers were sunbathing?"

Somehow I managed to answer, "Yes, ma'am."

Mother disappeared into the house and returned with a mile-high stack of tea-towels and my sewing basket. "Sit over here," she ordered, motioning toward a chair on the porch, "and begin working on these pieces. You are not permitted to leave the yard until every stitch is completed."

I took the linens from her and held them to my soggy body as I sat down. As slowly as I sewed, I knew I would still be in that chair when I was 103, cross-stitching my life away, my brittle gray hair falling over my eyes and blurring my vision.

I managed to sew until Jack had gone to do his chores, Hanna had gone inside to recover from her afternoon ordeal, and Mother, Papa, and Aunt Mittie had gone back to the Hopkinses'. Then I decided to get away from the farm for a while and get a breath of air that wasn't dirty with unfairness. I slipped to my room and changed clothes, then walked into the woods in the back of the house.

I didn't do anything to please any of them anyway. They would probably not notice I was gone. But there was something awry in my direction of flight, because at a turn I ran smack into the burial party taking Mrs. Hopkins to the cemetery.

Most of the people in the procession were on foot, strolling behind the black wagon that carried the body from the church to the graveyard. I could see Mother and Papa among the mourners. Mother was leaning against Papa's shoulder.

I stepped away from the road and sat down behind a bush to watch the procession stop at the cemetery.

Four men unloaded Mrs. Hopkins's casket and set it beside the readied grave. It was a plain pine box with oversized metal handles that looked as if they might once have been on a grain wagon. That stark white coffin was mellowed only by a large bouquet of wildflowers that some black-veiled woman laid on top of it.

They carried Mrs. Hopkins's husband to the gravesite then and seated him on a packing crate. Their children flocked around him, touching him and whimpering softly as Reverend Pike motioned for the crowd to gather closer for the parting words.

"We have come together today to honor Alta Hopkins, a pillar in our community," Reverend Pike began.

A mockingbird called from a sycamore beside the cemetery. First its cry was that of a thrush, then a robin, and finally the tweet, tweet of a cardinal.

Reverend Pike looked up and smiled toward Heaven. "Even as that bird, who is so pleasantly serenading us this afternoon, can be many birds rolled into one, so Alta was many women rolled into one. She was a devoted wife, a loving mother, and a hard worker."

Mrs. Hopkins's children stopped sniffling and stood up straight, obviously proud of their mother.

Reverend Pike turned toward Mrs. Hopkins's husband. "Of course, Gerald, no one knows better than you what a fine nurse Alta was. She took care of you after your war injury without complaint. She shouldered the responsibility of caring for your family."

Gerald Hopkins nodded slowly.

"Now she will expect you to carry on," Reverend Pike continued.

Mr. Hopkins said loudly, "I will."

Reverend Pike turned back to the crowd. "Of course, Alta does not leave this earth without contribution. She has fine children who will go on with their lives and be worthy members of this community. Alta will keep a watchful eye on them, Lord willing. Now she will have a time of rest, something she has been unable to have for many years. Rest in sweet peace in Jesus' arms."

Reverend Pike signaled for the pallbearers to lower the casket into the grave. When the casket was in the ground he threw a small shovel of dirt on it and said, "Ashes to ashes and dust to dust."

I knew Mother couldn't have known where I was hiding, but for some reason as the preacher said the final words, she looked my way, and I could almost feel her gaze piercing my soul. I wanted to run to her and touch her. If she died I didn't know what I would do. Especially if she died before I had the opportunity to get to know her better. We always seemed to be at odds. In disagreement over something. I felt as if I were losing more of her every day.

I slid back through the woods toward home, accompanied by the shrieks of bluejays and the sound of those little children mourning for their mother. Their dirty, tired, overworked poor mother I had served on our everyday dishes.

❋ The Pie Auction ❋

Jack was tickled pink because he was able to get Cousin Hanna to join him in his war against Lizzie Bingman. In the next week the two of them became as close as jam on bread. As far as I was concerned, their relationship was about as sticky.

Between spending my time practicing piano and working on the tea-towels Mother had assigned me for the swimming caper, I had very little time to worry about the devious plans of my enemies. By the end of the week and after a challenge from Hanna, I knew I should have been worrying.

On Saturday morning before the annual church pie auction and singing, Hanna floated into the kitchen dressed in a frilly yellow pinafore. She acted like a butterfly drunk on vinegar. She sat down prissily beside Mother and said, "Aunt Lana, I think it would be nice if Lizzie and I baked pies for tomorrow, too. After all, the church needs all the money it can raise to build those extra rooms, and it would mean less work for you and Aunt Mittie if Lizzie and I helped out."

Mother set the bowl of cookie dough she had been stirring on the table and answered, "Yes, that would be a wonderful thing for you girls to do."

I was peeling potatoes at the sink and pretended I didn't hear what Hanna said, hoping I would be excused. But I knew I was only wishing my troubles away, when Mother asked, "Lizzie, what kind of pies will you bake?"

Mud pies were the first kind that came to mind, but I held my tongue until I thought for a minute, then answered, "Pumpkin."

"That will be fine," Mother agreed. "There's plenty of pumpkin filling stored in the cellar."

Hanna cleared her throat dramatically and said, "Aunt Lana, I want to make cream pies. Coconut cream and lemon cream, if that's all right with you."

"That will be fine, dear," Mother said slowly.

I knew who Hanna was trying to impress — Jeffrey Wilson, the mayor's son — a stuck-up kid with legs like a sandpiper. He was the kind of boy who wouldn't kneel to shoot marbles because he might get his knickers dirty. Usually, Jack and Edman made faces at him behind his back, but since Hanna had come over to their side, they had been especially nice to old Jeffrey when he came calling on Cousin Dear.

Right after lunch, I made my pies. Their crusts were an inch thick and looked as if they would bow in the middle. The pumpkin looked all right when I put it in the oven, but the fire must have been too hot because the filling bubbled on top and burned a tarpaper black.

Hanna took one look at my pies and laughed like a

crow, shaking her blond curls and nearly popping the buttons off the front of her pinafore. She made me sick, and I was sick already, really sick. I felt sick to my stomach, as if I had eaten a basket full of green apples.

I left her laughing and poking fun at my burned offerings to the pie auction and went upstairs to my bed to lie down. After an hour, when I saw I wasn't going to feel much better, I moped down to the parlor and began to practice my piano. Mother had hinted that I might be called on to play the next day at the singing, and I needed all the practice I could get.

Halfway through the second verse of "Amazing Grace," Brother Edman joined me in the parlor. He plopped down on the floor, took the "P" encyclopedia from the bookcase, and loudly flipped through its pages.

On the fourth verse of the hymn, he looked up at me with his owl eyes and said, "That's the worst piano playing I've ever heard."

I kept on popping the keys and answered, "Thank you, Edman."

"Really. That's the sourest playing I've ever heard."

I stopped the accompaniment with a bang. "What do you suggest I do to improve it, Old Wise One?"

"Well, it says here," Edman began as he stood up and showed me a page in the book, "that sometimes the piano strings become too lax."

I stared at him.

"Too lax, too lax," he repeated shrilly. "Loose, baggy strings."

I smiled, "Well, surely no one wants baggy strings. What do we do?"

He didn't answer, but instead climbed up beside me on the piano bench and opened the top of the instrument, exposing a series of hammers and strings. "Amazing!" he exclaimed as he slipped a hand down behind the keyboard.

"Edman, are you sure you know what you're doing?"

He handed me the encyclopedia and began to dig around inside the piano with both hands. After about five minutes, he sat back, instructed me to close the lid, and walked across the room to shelve the book. With a quick wave he left me alone to do my practicing, mumbling something about my owing him a nickel.

I should have checked the piano before he left, but being the trusting person I was, I didn't. And the first chord I struck was silent. I had a touch like a bull dancing on eggs, but even pounding the hardest I could I couldn't get a sound out of the piano. Edman had certainly cut out the sour notes; he had cut out *all* of the notes.

I hurried to the kitchen to find him and have him fix his repair job. He wasn't in the kitchen, but Hanna was. Hanna and her blue ribbon pies. The meringue on her masterpieces stood two inches high and was toasted a delicate brown color. The crust around the edges was fluted perfectly and draped over the sides of the pans. What's worse was that she had them sitting beside my pies, which suddenly looked like two misplaced piles of manure.

"Your pies are beautiful," I said stiffly.

"Yes, they are," Hanna agreed, gently touching the meringue on one of them.

"They should impress Jeffrey," I volunteered.

"Yes, they will," she agreed again as she hurried out of the kitchen toward the staircase.

I sat down at the table and tried to think of a way to have my pies mysteriously disappear. If George wasn't on the enemy side, I would have asked him to help me, but I knew there was no use bothering him about it as long as Jack had a fist to his nose.

I stepped outside for only a moment to see if Mother was working in the garden. When I came back into the kitchen, I saw George, spoon in hand, dipping gingerly into one of Hanna's pies. Her other pie was already missing its crown of meringue and the one George was working on was half-eaten.

"George Thompson Bingman, what are you doing?" I screamed.

He looked at me, foaming at the mouth like a mad dog. "Eatin' pies," he mumbled.

"Those are Hanna's pies to take to the auction tomorrow," I tried to explain to the still-eating demon.

He gulped loudly and wiped his mouth on his sleeve. "Oh, no," he finally muttered when what I had said got through to his tiny, hard brain. "Oh, Lizzie, don't tell."

I knew I had him. The little monster in my power. "On one condition," I said slyly.

"Anything, anything," he agreed. At that point I thought he would have cut off his stubby toes if I'd asked him to.

"You help me make certain my pies don't get to the auction, and I'll help you repair Hanna's pies," I offered, pointing to my pumpkin creations.

George took a deep breath and exclaimed, "Those things are pies! I thought they were . . ."

"Shut up, George," I ordered as I hurried to the cabinet for a bowl. I was about to get the eggs for the meringue when I had a wonderful idea. If I was going to fix Hanna's pies, I might as well fix them good.

I found some alum, known for putting the pucker in pickles, and had George go upstairs to get Papa's shaving soap. Between the two products, a half dozen egg whites, and a little water, George and I made a beautiful meringue. I spooned the mixture onto the pies and popped them into the still warm oven until the soap settled.

"What do you think?" I asked George when I set the creations on the table.

"Look just like they did," he agreed, again picking up a spoon to taste the meringue.

"George! Remember that's soap," I yelled.

He laid down the spoon and, with his undergrown mind, ran outside to play.

Sunday morning I still felt sick to my stomach. I felt not only as if I'd eaten green apples, but also sour grapes washed down with a dose of vinegar. After I'd dressed in my best outfit, I helped Mother pack the pies. More than once she complimented Hanna on her artful baking. She didn't say one thing about my attempt.

In the wagon, I gave George the signal to dump my pies. He was so clumsy, we both knew he would get by with it. On command, he stepped onto the tailgate and caused the basket containing my pies to fall to the dirt. Their sorry-looking burned faces were buried an inch deep in the dust.

"George," I said flatly, "you have destroyed my pies."

Jack ran toward the wagon, a mean look on his face. He said, "George, what in the world have you done . . ." but when he saw whose pies were on the ground, he changed his tone of voice and said only to me, "At least they look better now."

I turned away from him as he walked to his courting buggy and headed toward town to pick up his beloved Rosie. I managed to smile to myself, barely listening to the lecture Mother gave George about watching where he was going. Score one point for Lizzie Bingman.

There were already thirty rigs at the church when we arrived. Husbands and sons were proudly carrying the pies their womenfolk had made to the display tables. There seemed to be dozens of apple cobblers, sprinkled with cinnamon; and plenty of lattice-topped cherry pies, creamy-faced custards, blueberry, raisin, strawberry, and rhubarb pastries. You name it, a pie by that name was there.

The men walked around the tables, looking at the baked goods and deciding which ones to bid on. Hanna's pies got a lot of attention. One old woman said enthusiastically about them, "That's the prettiest meringue I've seen in a coon's age."

Hanna smiled like an upside down rainbow and leaned

against Jeffrey's arm as he admired her baked wonders. He bent toward her and crooned mushy things into her pointy ear as he reached into his pocket to fish out a wad of bills. Jeffrey the Gallant.

Before the auction began, the preacher called everyone into the auditorium for a round of hymn singing. Amos Wheeler, who had a face like a toad, led the song service. We plodded through the hymns, "The Old Rugged Cross," "Standing on the Promises," "In the Sweet By-and-By" . . . I wasn't paying much attention to anything until Dottie Mitchel, the pianist, swooned. She was eight months with child and was dressed in a heavy wool gown that came practically to her toes. A couple of men caught her as she fell, and some of the ladies followed them outside. From the window I saw they had propped her against a shady tree and were giving her a good fanning.

Mother tapped me on the shoulder and said, "Lizzie, why don't you play the piano for us?"

"But . . . but . . . but," I stammered.

Before I could say anything more, Mother waved at Brother Wheeler and announced to the entire congregation, "Lizzie will play."

"I haven't had much time to practice," I told her.

"Nonsense, you had all day yesterday," she insisted.

I heard Edman snicker. Then I heard Jack utter a low, grumbly giggle. I knew then who had put Edman up to his prank, some big blowhard who was out in force to win a certain bet.

I stuffed all my courage into a wide smile and hurried to the piano. Unfortunately, my will power alone didn't produce a pianist. I sounded as if I were accompanying the singing while wearing mittens. All the time I was playing, I could hear George and Edman snickering behind me. After a couple of battered and butchered songs, Reverend Pike dismissed us to the auction. I was still sick to my stomach, and now I was sick at heart — my own family had laughed at me. It made me feel mean and mad.

Hanna's pies sold first. One went to Jeffrey, who paid for it then hurried outside with Hanna to sit on the front steps. The other pie sold, unfortunately, to the banker. He offered a piece to his wife. She took a bite of soap suds and began to gag and spit like a kid swallowing castor oil.

George started laughing like an idiot, running from Jeffrey, who I'd heard was laid out on the porch holding his throat, and the banker's wife, who was yelling at her husband like a Comanche.

Jack found me in the crowd and asked loudly, "Did you have anything to do with those bad-tasting pies?"

I felt really sick. "What if I did?"

He grabbed me by the arm and dragged me out to a tree beside the picket line. "What are you trying to do to your family? Embarrass the life out of us?"

My stomach hurt so bad, I didn't care what he said.

"We try to do right by you, but you just stab us in the back. Don't you, Lizzie?" He shook me hard.

Rosie walked toward us. Jack let go of me and hurried to her. He said loudly, "Come on, Rosie, I don't want you around *her*. Lizzie's a bad influence."

I felt as if someone had stepped on my heart. I leaned against a tree by Jack's rig and thought about mean things to do to him. On impulse, I removed the key peg that connected the horse to the buggy. When he and Rosie started home, the horse would have a head start.

I went to the Ladies' outhouse and shut the door. While I was perched over one of the holes, I suddenly knew why I'd been feeling sick. During the day I'd become a woman. "Come around," as Mother would say. Had my time of the month. I felt a funny sensation, kind of happy, kind of sad, and right then, worried. What was I going to do, stranded across the yard from church and my mother?

I sat there until Sally Fisher came out to use the toilet and asked her to please get me some help. In a moment, Mother was there with a concerned look on her face. "Is there something wrong, Lizzie?"

"I've come around, Mother," I answered shakily.

She smiled slightly and made me a pad out of some handkerchiefs she had in her purse. "Come along, now, and I'll take you home," she said. She helped me out of the toilet and motioned for Edman to come to her.

"Don't tell him, Mother," I pleaded.

She looked at me lovingly and said, "I wouldn't do that, Lizzie."

Edman walked over to Mother and gave me a questioning look. I simply smiled at him.

"What did you want, Mother?" he finally asked.

"Hitch up the team," she said. It was her no-nonsense voice.

"Where are we going?" he asked.

"You are staying here. Lizzie and I are going home." Mother extended her hand to me.

"I'll tell Papa I'm driving you," Edman said as he turned back toward the church.

"Son, I am perfectly capable of driving my own rig," Mother said curtly.

"You don't . . . need me?" Edman asked, his voice cracking.

"Of course I need you," Mother said as she motioned toward the wagon. "I need you to ready the team."

With the reins in Mother's hands we left Edman standing in the churchyard, kicking dust on his socks.

Mother didn't say anything to me on the ride home. Only when we were in the house did she slip an arm around me and take me upstairs to her bedroom.

We sat on her bed and Mother said, "Lizzie, there are some wonderful things about being a woman. Some very wonderful things."

I leaned against her and cried. Then we lay on her bed all afternoon with our arms around each other. It was a special time for us. Mother didn't even ask me about Hanna's pies or why my piano playing was so awful. She just held me, and I went to sleep thinking about what she had said about its being wonderful to be a woman — and thinking about how stupid Jack must have looked when the horse ran away without the buggy. I hoped he had gotten dumped on his proper behind.

* The Cigarette *

George took the blame for the soapy pies and got so busy confessing that he even said he was the one who "fixed" Jack's rig. I suspected Jack had threatened him and forced him to admit to the acts so that Mother wouldn't be embarrassed by my "unladylike" behavior. Edman felt so bad about my horrible musical performance that he, too, confessed, telling Papa about his repair work on the piano. Papa took them both to the woodshed when they got back from the pie auction. He must have really laid the strap to them because neither of them could sit down even at breakfast the next morning.

On Thursday of that week, Papa announced it was time for our annual trip to Joplin, the biggest city in southwest Missouri, so he could "settle up" with the companies he dealt with. What it meant was that he would go to town and receive his earnings from the shipping place where he sent his lead, meet with other mine owners to discuss business, and do his banking. We were to leave home the next day and were planning to stay in Joplin through the following Sunday.

Thursday afternoon, while Mother and Aunt Mittie

were packing for the trip, George and Edman burst into the kitchen with startled looks on their faces. Both of them were barefoot, filthy, and out of breath.

"What's wrong with you?" I asked, staring at Edman.

Edman leaned against a cabinet and mumbled, "It's him! He's got two of our broody hens."

George began to moan, kicking at the cabinet with his toes — the original five little piggies. "He'll eat 'em up. Feathers and all. Our poor baby chicks. They'll die. Turn toes up and croak."

I hurried to the stairs and called for Mother. She rushed into the kitchen and took the two squawling demons into her arms. "What is it, my little men?" she asked softly.

I thought I was going to throw up.

Edman took off his spectacles and wiped his brow, finally answering, "That tramp, old Slap Happy, got two of our mama chickens."

"He'll have them for dinner," George added. "We'll never be rich now."

I knew they didn't care a lick whether or not the hens got eaten. What they cared about was their profitable little chicks chilling in their shells.

Mother motioned for both boys to sit at the table and told me, "Get them some cool milk, please, Lizzie."

I served the whimpering tyrants while Mother got Jack from where he was working in his melon patch. He followed Mother into the kitchen and sat down between George and Edman.

Jack patted George on the arm and said, "I'll find old Slap Happy."

"You will?"

"I'll get your hens back so your eggs will hatch and you'll make your money."

I saw dollar signs return to George's eyes.

Jack stood up and said to Mother, "I'll go find the old tramp. He's probably at the creek."

I sat down at the table and said softly, "Slap Happy will still be in the woods. He doesn't go near the creek until almost dark."

Jack eyed me. "What are you talking about?"

"Slap Happy won't be near Shoal Creek until later when he goes down there to cook his supper," I explained.

"How do you know?" Mother asked, a suspicious glint in her eye.

"I just know," I said quietly.

Jack pounded the table in front of me. "Lizzie, you keep away from that grizzled old fool."

I looked up at Jack, but bit my lip before I said something that would get me in trouble with Mother.

"Yes, Elizabeth, stay away from him," Mother said shakily. "There's no telling what he might do to a young girl — alone. Heaven only knows all the riffraff he runs with."

Jack started out after the stolen chickens. He had a rifle tucked under his arm until Mother quietly took it from him, saying, "You won't need this."

"I'll be back by suppertime," he assured Mother, eyeing the confiscated gun as he backed out the door. "Just need to check along the creek."

"Slap Happy won't be there," I said to myself.

Truth of it was I had seen Slap Happy many times when I sneaked away to walk beside Shoal Creek. He always wore buckskin britches and a fringed jacket even in the thick summer heat. And usually he carried a hunting bow with him. I would be walking along, throwing stones in the water, and he would walk the bank opposite me or climb a tree and sit up there chattering like a squirrel. Other times he would mimic the coo of a dove or the howl of a coyote.

The story goes that Slap Happy was once a business-man in Neosho, a neighboring town. He had a bad turn of events in his life and some people said he was possessed by the Devil or became sick or just went plain crazy.

He never seemed that way to me. He seemed like a tired, unhappy old man.

When Jack returned home for his evening meal not having seen a glimpse of the tramp, I wasn't surprised. I had told him Slap Happy wouldn't be at the creek until near dark. Jack was about as bullheaded as a boy could be.

When Friday came, rain came with it. My brothers loaded our weekend luggage into the wagon and buggy and spirited us to the train depot for our trip to Joplin. Mother and Aunt Mittie wore oilcloth draped over their best bonnets. Hanna and I did the best we could to keep dry under a tarpaulin Jack had rigged up over the back of the wagon.

We arrived at the station just in time to get on board the Union Pacific before it began to sputter and spew along the tracks toward the city. The conductor walked back to us when we were settled and took our tickets from Papa. "Be in Joplin in a little over an hour," he told Papa, "if'n the creek don't rise." He laughed hoarsely as he waddled down the aisle to collect the other passengers' tickets.

Mother had gasped at the thought of the creek rising, but Papa reminded her there were no large creeks between Granby and Joplin. Finally, she settled back and, with Aunt Mittie, began to work on some crocheting they had brought along for their never-idle hands.

I had to sit on a greasy-feeling, leather-covered bench across from Jack and Edman. Hanna sat beside me. You would have thought they were all taking their last journey — maybe to the gallows — by the way their mouths turned down as if gravity was waging a private battle with each of them. I tried to start a conversation by saying, "It sure is raining cats and dogs."

Jack pulled out a copy of the *Granby Gazette* from his slicker pocket and began to read.

Edman started, "And it sure looks like —" but Jack elbowed him, and he quit talking and stared out the window.

Usually the trip to Joplin was fun. We would stay at Smith's Boarding House. It was a big, three-story hotel with fancy flowered wallpaper and a water closet. Mr. Smith was an old friend of Papa's, and he always made sure we got the best rooms in the house — a two-bedroom suite with a connected sitting room. Papa and the boys slept in one room, and we *ladies* slept in the other.

I liked the hotel beds. The headboards were carved

into dragons, and I usually pretended I was an Oriental princess being held for ransom by an evil prince.

Mother interrupted my daydreaming by offering me a sandwich and a pint-sized jar of lemonade. I took the food from her and began to eat.

"Hey, Lizzie, trying to look like an old cow chewing her cud?" George asked as he leaned over the seat between Jack and Edman. Jack popped him on the nose. The next time George poked his head over the seat, he opened his mouth widely and showed me a half-chewed piece of deviled egg. Before I could say anything, maybe tease him about his missing chickens, he ducked out of sight, leaving only the faint scent of egg yolk in the air.

We arrived at the boarding house and got settled in. At five o'clock we sat down to a supper of roast beef and mashed potatoes. The rain had lessened to a drizzle, and the general mood at the meal was festive. Jack even obliged and passed me the gravy. I pretended not to notice that he nearly poured it into my lap.

The rest of the evening was uneventful until we went to bed, at which time I was serenaded by the strange chorus of snores that came from Mother, Aunt Mittie, and Cousin Hanna. They sounded like frogs around the pond in summertime. I got out of bed, slipped to the window, and opened it to listen to the street sounds. Somewhere a baby was crying; and somewhere else, far away, I could hear the faint tinkling of piano keys.

It wasn't the kind of piano they had at church with huge white, flat keys or the kind of piano we had at home — ornate and polished, but it was a real barroom piano. I'd seen a picture of one in a pamphlet once,

advertising a show — FRED FERRING AND HIS FLYING FAIRIES
had been the billing. And that piano was plunking out
tunes like "Frankie and Johnny" and "My Melancholy
Baby."

Sometimes between the crowded chords I heard a
woman laugh. It wasn't a polite giggle, the only kind
Mother allowed even when something truly funny happened, like the time Jack got his drawers caught in the
milling machine and was stripped naked before he knew
what hit him. Instead, it was a full-bodied female laugh.
I could almost see the woman as she laughed —big-
bosomed, wearing high-topped, patent leather shoes
that hit below her knee-hemmed dress. Her gown was
probably red with a hint of black lace, and her hair was
whirled into raven-colored clouds, held in place by tiny,
jeweled pins.

Someone rolled over in bed, and I heard Mother say,
"Lizzie, shut that window and get some sleep."

I reluctantly pulled down the glass and crawled into
the full-feathered bed beside snoring Hanna. I tried not
to touch her cold, clammy feet and covered my ears so I
wouldn't have to listen to her wheezing.

The next morning, Papa left the hotel early to settle his
business. After that, he was meeting with some other
miners to discuss upcoming agreements between labor
and management. The "teamster talks," Papa called
them. And he hated dealing with anyone over giving
them more money. Mother always lectured him about
his duty to be generous, but usually his only response

was "Humph." We all knew when he returned from the meetings, he would be puffy-eyed and lock-jawed. Only Mother's soothing reassurance could calm him then.

Mother and Aunt Mittie were going to spend the day at the hospital. Mother wanted to see what was new in modern medicine and she hoped to get to speak with a doctor or two about extending their services to Granby. She called us to her and said, "You may go exploring, but you must stay in this neighborhood. There are things in this city, well, I wouldn't even want you to *dream* about."

During Mother's speech, George was cracking his knuckles and grinning like the cat that ate the canary.

The moment Mother left us on our own, Jack grabbed the little monster by his shirt collar, nearly ripping it off as he said, "George Bingman, you stay out of trouble. And I mean it!" Jack flashed me a warning look as he and Edman hurried across the street to the drugstore. They were probably going to fill up on malteds and cherry fizzes.

"What a fine couple of brothers," George said to me, a hurt tone to his voice.

"You can say that again," I agreed.

"What a fine couple of brothers," he repeated.

I quickly left George standing alone with his mouth open, so I could stroll down the sidewalk, window shopping at the dress stores. I was counting my blessings that Hanna had decided the hot sun would be too much for her and that she would retire to the front porch of the boarding house for the day.

As I walked along I could hear George scuffling

behind me. He was dragging a stick or something along the wooden sidewalk. I glanced back at him in time to see Jack's bossy face at the window of the drugstore. He was watching to see where George and I were going — the dear.

As I waved mockingly to Jack, George rushed to me. "Can I go with you, Lizzie? I'll be good."

I continued to look at Jack as I answered, "Sure, George. Would you like to do something really daring?"

George's eyes lit like the first evening star.

"Would you walk with me down to the row?"

"Where the music and bars are?" he asked, his little mule ears flapping.

"We'll take a look around and come right back."

He took a quick look at Jack, who was still at the drugstore window. Jack waved his fist at the little darling. That made George mad, and he answered, "I'll go with you. You bet I will."

The trip to the row was a longer walk than I had figured — a good twenty blocks across town. We had to stop halfway there and buy a fruit ice and take a rest. I made the mistake of letting George have the first sip of the drink. He sucked up the flavoring like a skinny tick lunching on a fat hound.

After our treat, we plodded along until the whole atmosphere of the town changed. The buildings were soot covered. Under the black icing I could see traces of red brick or white Carthage stone. There was also a scattering of tarpaper shacks and sheds. The smells on the other side of the tracks were unusual, too. Something like a cross between an outhouse and the cellar after the apples had been wrapped and stored there for winter.

We sat down on a door stoop and listened to the street noises for a few minutes. On a second-story landing a dried-up weed of a woman was hanging what I supposed was her laundry out to dry. Mother would have thrown the entire washing into the rag bag, but the woman up there was pinning each garment to the line with great care.

Below the woman on the main floor porch, a cob-eared farmer sat on a three-legged stool tipped back against the building. Smoke was swirling around his face from a big-based pipe he was sucking. When he saw us staring at him, he held up the pipe as a wave.

George waved back, then shot me a look asking whether or not he should have.

"They're just people, George," I said confidently, then wondered if that had been a fair judgment when the man looked up at the laundry woman and began to curse a blue streak at her about how her wet drawers were dripping down and putting out his smoke.

I grabbed George by his arm and dragged him down the street. We kept getting farther and farther into the jungle of alleys and door stoops and shacks. From behind a pile of garbage, a big, cross-breed mutt came at us, the hair bristled on his back.

"Here puppy, here, boy," George called like an idiot. He knelt down and waited for the snarling dog to come to him for a pat on the head.

I was about to scream at my sorry-brained brother to
take off running, when the dog surprised me and slunk
over to George and let him run his stubby fingers
through its yellow-colored fur.

"They're just dogs, Lizzie," George reminded me,
with the same air of confidence I had used before.

I would have taken George, the friend of the beasts,
and headed back to the boarding house, but suddenly
the air was filled with the rich sound of a ragtime piano.
The first hard beats eased into a ballad — a slow,
mournful tune that went in my ears, circled my heart,
and made me want to hum along.

"Come on, George," I ordered, pulling at his pudgy
arm.

He followed me to a glass-fronted bar with the words
TARWATER SALOON painted on the window. I cupped my
hands around my eyes and peeked inside. The player at
the piano was a big black man with graying hair. His
fingers never hit a key directly, but instead skimmed
over the tops of them, barely telling them to move.

A noise called my attention to the door, and a deep-
honey voice asked, "What you youngens doin' out
here?"

The voice was that of the woman I had imagined from
the boarding house window. She wasn't wearing the red
and black dress, but her hair was piled high the way I'd
thought it would be, and her face had a certain knowledge of the world about it.

George smiled real big and looked the woman over
from head to foot as if he was planning to buy her.

"Wanna see my teeth, honey?" the woman asked him, chuckling.

George answered, "Yeah," and would have gone over to peer into her mouth if I hadn't caught him by his shirt.

"Excuse us, ma'am," I said quickly as I turned around and pulled George with me.

"Wait a minute, wait a minute," the woman called after us. "Come on in and have a root beer."

"Inside?" I asked, turning toward her.

"Sure," she said, smiling widely. "No one here but me and old Hank."

Before I could make up my mind about whether or not to accept her invitation, George was beside the woman, actually holding her hand and letting her lead him inside. I decided that men were basically weak-willed.

George even let her lift him up onto a bar stool. I slipped to a seat beside him and said, "Your tongue's hanging out, brother dear," as the woman fixed our drinks.

When she brought us our fizzes, she introduced herself. "My name's Dixie Crane," she drawled. "Who are you kids?"

"I'm George Thompson Bingman, and this kid is my sister, Lizzie."

"Pleased to meet you, ma'am," I said stupidly.

Dixie pulled a stool up beside us and began all the usual conversation about who our parents were, where we were from, nothing really important until she asked me, "What would your mama say if she knew you two were here?"

The thought of it hit George while he had a mouth full

of root beer. He spit wildly and drizzled the mirror behind the bar with a warm spray.

Dixie laughed and pulled a long, ready-rolled smoke from her bosom. She begged a light from the old man at the piano, and puffed on the tobacco until its end was a flaming red.

George was staring at her like the face on a Halloween jack-o-lantern.

"Want a puff?" Dixie asked George, holding the cigarette toward him.

He formed his lips into a pucker and gave the smoke stick a good draw. First to go was the pucker. His lips flattened out as if they had been run over by a wagon. Then his nose began to run, and his eyes blinked like those of a frog on a lily pad. And from somewhere in his chest a rumble started and grew until it escaped by way of his mouth with an explosive cough.

"Liked it, huh?" Dixie asked.

Green-faced George managed to answer, "Yes, ma'am."

"Want a puff?" Dixie asked me. The thought of a woman smoking made my head rattle. Suddenly, the whole bar seemed hot and sulfurous.

"Maybe another time," I said, trying to sound womanly.

"In that case, take one with you," Dixie offered, handing me a cigarette. "Nice to have met you kids. I have to get to my business now." She excused herself by saying, "Feel free to take your time and finish your drinks."

I reached for my glass and found it was empty. George

had finished it off and was drinking everything in sight. He was still gagging and spitting halfway back to the boarding house.

I took the special gift from Dixie and put it between my newly swelling breasts. It was cradled safely there. I planned to smoke it, but I wanted to be alone when I did, especially if I ended up acting like George.

All the next week Mother pouted while doing her work. The miners had awarded the teamsters a raise of nearly three percent, so she couldn't say that Papa hadn't fulfilled his duty to be generous. Since the teamsters were from out of town, however, the money they earned would not be spent in Granby. Business was lost as was extra income for the mine owners and, in turn, the miners. That meant the Citizen and Community Advocates would receive less in contributions for community projects. And, according to Mother, what money they did have had already been forwarded to the proper authorities to put in electricity. That would put plans to start a clinic on hold for at least another year. A year, Mother felt, was much too long to wait, especially after she had seen all the miracles awaiting the sick at the hospital in Joplin.

As Mother prepared to go on her regular visiting rounds that Wednesday, she saw two wagons approach our house. She called us kids onto the porch and asked if any of us knew who they were.

Jack looked at his feet as he answered, "Papa told me before he went to the smelter this morning that the electricity crew might be out before he got back for lunch."

"What are they doing?" Mother asked shrilly as a couple of the men bounded out a wagon and began to dig at the edge of the yard.

"They're putting in a pole for the wire," Jack explained.

Mother put her hands on her hips and turned quickly to stomp into the house. She appeared a few minutes later, wearing her bonnet, and had Jack load her baskets of goodies into the back of the buggy. He drove her past the electric men.

Jack waved politely to them. Mother looked straight ahead as if they weren't even there.

When they were gone Edman hitched up the wagon to drive Aunt Mittie and Hanna into town to do the week's shopping. I was to watch after George, but he begged so persistently to go with them that Aunt Mittie gave in. The last I saw of them, George was sitting on the tailgate of the wagon, sticking his tongue out at me.

It was the moment I had been waiting for — the chance to try the cigarette. I hurried to the barn and climbed into the loft, accompanied by a tin box full of kitchen matches and a bottle of vinegar. I'd heard Jack say once that some boys had smoked grapevine down at the creek and had used vinegar as a mouthwash so their folks wouldn't suspect anything.

I pulled a crate to the loft window and sat down on it. Then I took the cigarette out of my camisole. The tobacco was a bit limp from being carried in my bosom during the entire visit to Joplin, but it still promised an adventure.

I lit the cigarette quickly and let it burn until an ash formed. I took a long, slow puff. It didn't taste too bad. I decided that George had a fragile stomach. The second puff I took was a little headier, but I still managed to blow out the smoke. Halfway through the cigarette, I considered myself a professional pervert and made the horrible mistake of inhaling deeply and sending a mouth-load of smoke into my lungs.

I began to cough and gag as if I had the pleurisy and I dropped the cigarette on the hay-strewn floor. I tried to stomp it out, but I missed and a fire lit quickly and spread across the loft to a stack of straw stored against the back wall.

I opened my mouth to scream, but all I could do was cough out a weak-sounding Help. I grabbed a feedsack from the floor and beat at the fire, but the flames jumped higher.

I ran to the loft window and yelled, "I need help!"

There was no one around, not even the electric crew that had been working on the pole near the lane. All I could hear were the hens cackling loudly.

I felt that odd sensation you get when you think you're falling in a dream. I turned back to the fire. It was beginning to roar and looked as if it was lashing out at me. Once more I called into the sweet, cool air at the loft window, "Help me, please!"

There was movement in the yard. A wretched-looking face peeked around the corner of the coal shed.

It was Slap Happy. He had a gunny sack with him and by the wiggling going on inside it, I knew he had borrowed another couple of George and Edman's broody hens.

Slap Happy stood for a long moment looking toward the barn. Then he threw down the bag and hurried to the well. He filled a bucket with water and, pail in hand, maneuvered a ladder to the loft window. He climbed quickly to where I was waiting.

"Put it on the fire," he said breathlessly, passing the pail through the window.

I turned toward the flames and had to step back against the wall because the heat had become so great. Then, with a final breath of fresh air, I took a step forward and threw the water on the straw.

By the time I turned back to the window, Slap Happy was there with another bucket. I took the bucket from him and passed him the one I had emptied. Then I took that scary step back toward the fire and flung the water on it again. A great hiss sounded through the loft.

I don't remember how many buckets of water Slap Happy and I passed back and forth, but it must have been forty or fifty. The palms of my hands were blistered, partly because of the scraping metal of the heavy buckets' handles and partly because of the smoldering straw I had beat out with my hands as it threatened to ignite the hem of my dress.

"I think it's out," I called to Slap Happy.

He set down the bucket he was carrying and climbed the ladder. After hoisting himself through the window, he carefully kicked the straw around with his leather-covered foot. Without a word he walked to the ladder and motioned for me to follow him.

He would not take a step until I was in his arms, and I was thankful for the feel of his strong arms against my waist as I backed down the ladder. We stumbled arm-in-arm to the shade of a maple to cool off.

After we had caught our breath, I asked, "Could I get you something to drink?"

Slap Happy shook his head no.

"It's the least I could do," I said. "Thank you for helping me." I shuddered to think about what might have happened if the whole barn had caught fire.

He smiled a nearly toothless smile and stood up to leave.

I got up quickly. "Don't go. Stay for a hero's supper."

He shook his head no and started toward the woods.

"Wait," I called after him when I saw the sack he had left on the ground. The hens inside it were squawking to beat the band. I picked up the bag and carried it to Slap Happy. "You forgot your dinner."

"I'm not a thief," he said weakly.

"Consider it payment for the help," I told him.

Slap Happy smiled and took the bag, then he disappeared into the thick timber beyond the barn.

I turned to see Jack running toward the back yard. He didn't bother to open the gate, but jumped it and landed like a frog on a lily pad.

"Men, men, men, at the electric company," he exploded, waving his finger toward the road, "men said there was smoke coming from this way." He bent over double and breathed with his mouth open. When he finally stood up he asked, "What's going on?"

I looked at my blackened hands and seared dress. "Loft fire," I said weakly. When Jack took a step toward the barn, I added, "It's out."

Jack ignored my information and hurried to the barn and up the ladder to the loft. When he didn't come back down I climbed up after him. I found him sitting against the saved straw with his knees drawn up to his chin.

"I guess I was lucky I got it put out," I offered.

Jack didn't say anything.

"Not a lot of damage, I guess," I said.

Jack looked at me with a drawn face. "Lizzie, I found these." He held the vinegar bottle and the charred tin of matches toward me. "How could you do something like this?"

"You boys have all smoked —"

"Don't start, Lizzie." From his tone I knew he meant it. "You've gone too far. I don't think there's any way of getting you back."

I felt as if I'd been arrested, tried, and sentenced to hang at sunrise. "I'll tell Papa when he gets home," I said shakily.

"No!" Jack yelled.

"But —"

"But nothing! You are *not* taking the blame for this!"

"I don't understand. Shouldn't you be happy I'm about to meet the executioner?" My voice was shriller than I had planned.

"You are not going to shame Mother. You can play the part of the tart if you want, I guess. I can't stop you. But,

Lizzie, you are not going to drag our mother's good name through the mud for the sake of a cheap thrill."

"Are you finished?" I asked Jack's red face.

He grabbed hold of my shoulders and gave me a quick shake like a cat does a rat. "*You* are finished. I am in charge now. I will think of a story to explain all this, and, Lizzie, by golly, you'd better go along with it."

The rest of the evening was a nightmare. Jack told everyone Slap Happy stole the chickens and the adults put two and two together and came up with the conclusion it must have been Slap Happy who started the fire in the loft. The sheriff issued a warrant for the old man's arrest. I felt as if I had slipped the noose I deserved around a dear friend's neck.

I kept my mouth shut, partly because I began to think maybe Jack was right. Maybe I didn't have the right to shame Mother. I thought about that all evening, then faced the truth. I didn't really care so much about shaming anyone. I cared about my own hide. I was simply afraid to tell the truth because of Papa's fierce temper.

I went to bed with hair that smelled like singed chicken skin and a hollow burning in my chest. All I seemed to have gotten from being a worldly woman was toasted lungs, cindered tresses, and the privilege of feeling greener than a pea.

❋ The Kiss ❋

The fifth of August was my fifteenth birthday. It was also Jack's seventeenth birthday. Mother made plans to make the day a celebration to remember, as she did every year. Because of our identical entries into the world, two years to the minute, it was usually a day when Jack and I felt the closest as brother and sister — and as friends.

I knew this year was going to be different when, at our family birthday breakfast, Jack didn't even speak to me. Absentmindedly, I reached out and sniffed a trailing lock of my hair to see if it still smelled like smoke. It had been almost two weeks since the loft fire, and I had used everything from cider to egg yolks on my hair to get rid of the smell, but I could still sniff the faintest hint of tobacco. I began to think it was my conscience doing the smelling instead of my nose.

For that afternoon, Mother and Papa planned a birthday party for Jack and me. It was more of a social event. All of us kids got to invite guests. Hanna invited Jeffrey, but he said he couldn't come. They hadn't gotten along very well since he had tasted her cooking.

Edman invited the scholars of the town. One of them was a little boy who had won the seventh grade spelling contest last year. I assumed that Edman thought he was intelligent. His other guest was a girl two years older than he who talked with a nasal accent. Edman told Mother and Papa that she was from France. Her voice sounded to me as if she came from northwest Arkansas.

George invited Willy Avers and Petey Davis, both total idiots. Willy would be in the third grade for the second time come fall, and Petey was known to wet his pants when he got excited. George sure could pick the friends, but then I figured no normal person would be friendly to lame-brain George.

Jack invited only Rosie. I worried all morning whether or not he would tell her to keep away from me again as he had at the pie auction, especially since my smoking prank.

Not one brother asked me who I had invited, so I didn't volunteer the information. I could tell by the way they all stood around in their new striped pants, rocking back and forth on their heels, that they had a pretty good idea that Teddy Hargrove was my chosen guest.

At three o'clock, the guests began to arrive. George gathered his two fellow stupids to him and ran off toward the smokehouse, probably to think of rotten things to do to everyone else. Edman showed his company into the parlor, and all three of them stood around the encyclopedia case, no doubt solving the problems of the world. Jack, with Rosie, helped Mother in the dining room.

The decorations for the party supper were beautiful. Mother and Aunt Mittie had outdone themselves for the celebration. Mother had used daisies for the theme, and bowls of them were scattered around the house. A giant bouquet of black-eyed Susans and other field flowers sat majestically as a centerpiece on Mother's best lace tablecloth.

Just as Jack called everyone to the front yard for a game of croquet before dinner, Teddy arrived on his gray and white spotted appaloosa. Teddy looked just fine, dressed in a white suit with a pink shirt that had the texture of floss candy.

"Good day, Miss Lizzie," Teddy said gallantly as he slipped from the saddle and led his steed to the hitching rack. In one hand he carried a corsage of gardenias and in the other hand he had a gaily wrapped gift.

"Thank you, Teddy," I said loudly when he pressed the present into my opened arms. "It's wrapped beautifully."

Jack walloped a croquet ball across the yard.

Teddy ignored everyone else and guided me by the elbow into the house so he could pay his respects to Mother and Papa. Mother seemed to be a little cold toward him, but Papa put his arm around Teddy's shoulders and said kindly, "So nice you could come, son. I hope you have an appetite. Mrs. Bingman has prepared her famous veal loaf and all the fixings, and, of course, her delicious apricot sherbet for dessert."

Teddy appropriately smacked his lips and nodded his appreciation to Mother and Aunt Mittie. Mother almost smiled, then stiffened, probably remembering my red, white, and blue mess dress from the Fourth of July.

The croquet game Teddy and I joined was boring. Edman's girl friend giggled a lot. Rosie got hot in the afternoon sun and had to recover in the porch swing. And George and his demon buddies swiped half the croquet balls when Jack and Edman weren't looking. Only the call to supper saved us from social disgrace.

At the dining table, George and company acted decent, mostly because Papa sat beside George. Edman graciously escorted his friends to the table and solemnly seated them as if they were dining with the Queen of England.

By some total error in social planning, Mother seated Rosie between Jack and Teddy. Jack wanted to swap places with his girl so Teddy couldn't even brush her sleeve — I could tell by his red cheeks and fisted hands — but he knew Mother would have a fit, so he sat quietly, trying to look like a proper birthday boy.

We managed to finish eating the veal loaf, hot rolls and butter, creamed peas, mashed potatoes and gravy, corn, relish, baked apples, deviled eggs, blackberry jelly, strawberry jam, apricot sherbet, and angel food cake without incident, but when Mother served the coffee and mints, Teddy made the mistake of offering to pass Rosie the sugar bowl, and Jack flared like a lit stick of dynamite.

"Keep to yourself, Hargrove," Jack yelled. He jumped up and dragged part of the lace tablecloth with him.

Before Papa could tell Jack to sit down, Teddy was on

his feet, saying, "I was just being friendly, Bingman!"
He leaned toward Rosie.

I wanted to grab Teddy's sleeve and pull him down so
hard he would slide under the table.

Papa roared like a freight train, "You boys, remember
you are gentlemen. Jack, you are being a poor host, and,
Mr. Hargrove, you are being a poor guest."

Both boys stared at each other for a long minute, then
sat back down. Rosie looked as if she was going to faint
into her café au lait, and I heard Mother sigh like a
deflated balloon.

Jack and Teddy's private battle continued during the
party games, especially when there were no adults
present. On the treasure hunt, Teddy tripped Jack. On
the identifying-smells-while-blindfolded game, Jack
stuffed a piece of liver up Teddy's nose. And during the
singing they tried to out-bellow each other.

Later, while Jack and I unwrapped presents, Teddy
sat to the side and guffawed every time Jack got a gift
that seemed effeminate or childish. I knew Jack was near
tears when he opend a box from Papa's aged Aunt
Bernice and saw that it was a pair of winter drawers, two
sizes too small. He tucked them into their box and tried
to hide the gift under his chair, but Mother demanded
that he show the present to the guests and, in utter
humiliation, Jack had to wave his white flannels at the
crowd like a flag of surrender.

Teddy had brought me a five-pound box of chocolates.
Not the cheap kind from the candy bins at the mercantile, but a fancy brand in a gold box, with each piece set

in an individual foil cup on a layered tray. He told me his mother had bought the candy in Kansas City when she had gone up there to visit his father while he was on a business trip.

Hanna, who had remained anonymous for most of the party, suddenly came to life and walked toward me and my candy, smacking her rosebud lips. "Well, Mr. Hargrove, you certainly brought Lizzie a fine gift," she crooned.

Teddy stammered around for a minute, looking deep into Hanna's eyes. Too deep to suit me, so I dragged him away, handing my candy to Mother to be put aside.

In years past, all my brothers had pooled their money to buy me a really special gift. I knew there wouldn't be one after the bet — at least I hadn't found it anywhere. So the two shirts I had made for Jack stayed hidden in the bureau in my bedroom, and the fancy silver buckle I had ordered from Sears, Roebuck for him, well, I planned to send it back, or maybe give it to Teddy.

As the sun set, Mother served the final treats, salted peanuts and lemonade, and gave out the favors. She and Aunt Mittie had made sacks out of red and white wrapping paper and had filled each bag with a variety of stick candy. The guests finished their treats and took their gifts with them as they got ready to leave.

Teddy stayed behind the others and led me to the back porch. We stood beside the rose trellis. He pulled me close to him. "You look beautiful tonight, Lizzie. Beautiful as you always do."

I blushed, finally managing to say, "Thank you."

"Did you like my gift?" he asked earnestly.

"The candy was really nice. Thank you again."

"Is a 'thank you' all I get?"

I thought maybe he wanted more stick candy.

Teddy moved against me. "I was expecting more for my candy. You know, I give you something sweet, you give me something sweet in return."

"Like what, Teddy?" I asked, moving away from him.

"Like this," he said. He pulled me to him again and bent down to kiss me on my upturned lips.

I closed my eyes when I felt the soft touch of his mouth on mine, then, as in a sentimental novel, I felt a rush of wind and imagined a flash of fire. I had no idea that the rush and flash were at the hand of Jack, until I opened my eyes. Jack had hold of Teddy by the sleeve of his new suit, shaking him viciously.

"Get inside, Lizzie!" Jack ordered.

I didn't move.

Jack reached out and gave me a shove toward the house. I nearly fell down under the push.

"Jack Bingman, who do you think you are?" I started.

"Don't sass me, missy," he yelled as he dragged Teddy toward the barn lot. "You do as I say."

There was something about Jack's voice, a roughness, that made me turn quickly and sprint to the house. I flew inside, shut the back door with a bang, and hurried into the dining room to find Mother. When I stepped toward the table, my younger brothers and a couple of leftover guests jumped out and yelled, "Surprise, Lizzie!"

I could see a beautiful rocking chair sitting beside the hutch. It was draped in red and white ribbons.

"From your brothers," Edman said proudly.

Tears filled my eyes.

"Where's Jack?" Edman asked.

"Oh, he's coming," I whispered.

"Like the chair, Lizzie?" Edman asked, sounding more like the Edman I used to know — rather than Edman, the brother of the junior suffragette.

"It's beautiful, boys, really."

"Jack picked it out —" Edman began, but the group's attention was called away from his speech to the door as Jack stepped into the dining room. Jack looked a little mussed, but he quickly smoothed his shirt and ran his fingers through his hair. He threw me a look that was as heavy as a lead barrel.

Edman left my side and walked over to Jack. They whispered to each other for a while. Edman finally turned toward me and gave me the same heavy look Jack had thrown my way. I felt as if I'd grown ten feet tall and had the word *guilt* stamped on my forehead.

I started to walk over to them to thank them for the rocker and to apologize about the way I had been acting, when I heard Edman ask Jack, "How's Teddy now?"

Jack answered, "Well, his suit sure isn't white anymore."

He said the line real loud, so I'd be sure to hear it. I turned on my heels and padded across the room. I took the box of candy Teddy had given me from the shelf where Mother had placed it and sat down in my new chair. I intended to rock and eat until I was so fat I couldn't get up. Then all of my brothers would feel bad about the way they were treating me.

When I opened the candy box, I saw there wasn't a piece left. Every chocolate cream, every nut-filled confection, every jelly-topped mint was missing. With a quick look across the room, I caught a glimpse of George's face. He was whistling to himself and looking toward the ceiling, his grubby, thieving hands held behind his back. I started toward him, but he smartly walked over to stand between Jack and Edman, so I sat down and rocked.

I couldn't stop thinking about how Teddy's lips had felt when he kissed me. They were warm and smooth, not what I had expected from a boy. And what that kiss had done to me, I didn't even have words for. It was as if my brain was turned to applesauce and my skin actually crawled with goosebumps like the time I had the fever. I was afraid that a lot of Jack's harping about the differences in the temperaments of men and women was right. Somehow I couldn't deny the feeling I had that Teddy had an advantage over me. I wasn't sure I liked it one bit.

But as I ran my hand over the arm of the rocker it felt warm and smooth and sturdy like Teddy. Maybe I did want another kiss if even just to prove to myself I didn't like it.

Although I couldn't decide if I ever wanted Teddy to touch me again, I did know one thing. Every time I sat in the rocker I planned to remember his kiss by the rose trellis, *not* my hot-tempered brothers who had bought the chair for me.

I pulled my rocker to a window and sat there until everyone else had gone to bed, thinking mostly and making plans for my future. I even made a birthday wish on a star. I hardly thought it possible for it to come true, but at nine o'clock, George flew down the stairs, his knobby knees peeking out from under his yellow muslin nightgown. I had the privilege of hearing him fight open the front door and throw up over the porch railing, disposing of every bite of stolen chocolate.

* The Hurdy-Gurdy *

By the middle of August I could catch the faintest hint of autumn in the air. It would be right before dusk when the whippoorwills and other nightbirds began their mournful calling. What I smelled must have been the bittersweet scent of nearly formed walnuts or the musky aroma of prairie hay left to winter in the fields.

Whatever caused me to forget the heavy heat of the summer afternoons and turn my thoughts to cozy fires in the potbelly stove and fresh cider gushing from ripe apples also brought me the first true sign of the coming fall: the advertisements for the Longman Circus and Medicine Show.

The posters announcing the coming troupe had been tacked up throughout town and about the countryside by every boy in the community who was big enough to swing a hammer. Mr. Longman, the manager of the shows, rewarded all his young advertisers with free tickets to his concessions, and he never had to search very far for willing participants.

George and Edman had got in on the poster brigade. Mother had put a stop to their wild hammerings when she found a couple of the shiny handbills tacked up inside the house. Four more were flapping on the front fence. And the barn had been papered with pictures of snake charmers and clowns and dancing bears.

My little brothers didn't really mind the lecture they got for their overenthusiasm; instead, they spent their time running between home and the train depot, waiting for word about when the Longman shows would arrive in town.

On the twentieth of August, George rushed into the kitchen. His freckled face was blotched with heat and his wild red hair was standing up as if he had just had a good scare. He announced dramatically, "The medicine show is coming from Neosho."

The medicine show always came by wagon a couple of days before the circus. The remainder of the Longman shows came by train. Papa said they sent the first group ahead to stir up excitement and loosen everyone's purse strings.

Some of the superstitious country women made their children stay in their yards when the medicine show passed their farms.

"Take boy babies, them gypsies do," I'd heard many a calico-wrapped mother say from her front porch, her children peeking out from behind her apron like chicks from under a hen.

The procession always came past our place, and I delighted in seeing it. The medicine show people were a wild-looking group. Some of the women wore great, gold-colored loop earrings and brightly patched skirts that whirled around their ankles as they paraded behind the wagons.

The Longman group had come to Granby for each of my fifteen years, and most of the people in the show were familiar to me: there was Wild Man Apache who threw knives at pretty girls; the lady wrestlers who had more muscles than all the farm boys in Newton County combined; the Japanese jugglers and sword throwers; and the selection of freaks — Douglas the Dog-faced Boy, Bertie the Bearded Lady, and my favorite, Baby Ethel.

Baby Ethel was the same age that I was. She had been with the show for the last six years, and we had become friends. Baby Ethel weighed nearly four hundred pounds. For her show, she dressed in infant's clothing and crawled around in a giant-sized bassinet. It seemed to be humiliating to me to ask a grown-up girl to wear a baby bonnet and suck on a bottle, but Ethel had told me many times that she thought of it only as a job and that she was darn lucky to have it. She had no family, and without a means of support, no doubt she would have ended up as a ward of some poorhouse.

Papa always got a supply of free tickets for the shows since he played in the Miners Band and they entertained the crowds in front of the show tents to help the performers draw an audience. I usually took my share of the free passes and spent my time visiting with Baby Ethel when she wasn't entertaining a customer.

When the troupe passed our front porch, Baby Ethel saw me and waved. I waved back and yelled that I would be in town to see her.

The next afternoon, I went to Granby with Papa while he helped set up the bandstand. When I got the opportunity to slip away, I found Baby Ethel in her tent washing out her undergarments.

"Hello, Lizzie Bingman. How you doing?" Baby Ethel yelled when I pulled back the canvas. She took me into her arms, nearly crushing me.

"I'm fine, Ethel, and you?" I asked politely.

"As well as can be expected," she said, sighing. She began to wring out her washing. I noticed she was exceptionally pale.

When she saw my concerned look, she said, "It's the heat that makes me feel so bad, I guess."

"Why don't you get out of this hot tent for a while and sit under a shady tree?"

"Oh, I couldn't, Lizzie. I couldn't sit outside in public like that, not like regular folks."

"Why not?"

"See, Lizzie, it's all right, I mean my size and all, if people are paying me to see it, but to parade around *among* people, well, that wouldn't be proper. It would shame me."

I felt embarrassed for being so insensitive and hurriedly pulled a ticket Papa had given me from my pinafore pocket, holding it toward Baby Ethel.

"Not you, not you," she said in a flutter. "You're my friend, Lizzie. You don't pay. I didn't mean that." She stopped talking and looked me in the eye. "Your friendship means a lot to me. I don't have many friends."

Baby Ethel had said that to me before — last year — and as it had then, it broke my heart. I wanted to hold her hand and take her home and share my family with her. Having a family was what she wanted most in life; you could see it in her eyes.

"The circus is my family," she said suddenly, mostly to herself. "The circus is my family."

I nodded that I understood and helped her sort her clothing while we visited the afternoon away. I didn't leave her side until I heard Papa calling me to go home.

At supper, the boys seemed unusually quiet. I could almost see sneakiness in their eyes. Jack didn't once look directly at Mother, and Edman nearly had heart failure when Papa asked him what he and Jack had done in town that afternoon.

It wasn't until later that evening when Teddy stopped by to sit on the front porch with me that I found out why the boys looked as if they had just avoided being caught with their fingers in the sugar bowl.

Teddy puffed up like a hot biscuit and said, "Yes, ma'am, Lizzie, it was the greatest thing I've ever seen."

"What was, Teddy?" I asked, curiosity nearly pickling my brain.

"The hurdy-gurdy."

"What? I've peeked into the hurdy-gurdy show. Old Uriah Weeks cranks an organ while some jugglers or acrobats perform. I never thought it was much of a —"

"It was different this year," Teddy said breathlessly. "There were all these women, at least five. They were on this little stage with the lamps burning low. It was something!"

"Five women on a dark stage was something?" I thought maybe the sun had melted Teddy's noodle.

"They were dressed only in their underwear!"

"You're fibbing to me."

"No, really! And not drawers like our mothers hang out on the clothesline either. Real fancy ones — barely anything to them." He stopped talking and wiped the sweat from his brow. "Nearly naked they were. Those women were almost in their birthday suits . . ."

I signaled for him not to tell me any more. "Why would men pay to see barely dressed women?"

Teddy looked at me as if I'd slapped him. "Oh, come on, Lizzie. You *know* why men would pay for that. And two bits, to boot."

"I assume Jack and Edman were at the performance?" I asked casually. I couldn't imagine my tightwad brothers dishing out two bits apiece to see girls in their underwear.

"Not *the* performance," Teddy answered smugly. "All *three* of them."

"I don't believe either of them would pay seventy-five cents to see *anything*."

"It was worth it."

"I'd give my eyeteeth to see that show," I said. "But Papa hasn't given me any money yet."

"Oh, Lizzie, it isn't a show for *girls* to see. They don't allow women inside."

"To see other women?"

"No-o-o-o-o," Teddy answered nervously, shaking his head.

"I don't believe a word you've said. You're making all this up to make me mad."

"Ha! You come with me tomorrow afternoon and I'll prove it to you."

"How will you do that?"

"Just meet me behind your barn about one o'clock, and I'll show you," he promised as he slipped out and mounted his horse for the ride home.

After lunch the next day I had to help Aunt Mittie peel some early ripened apples. We sat on the back porch for the longest time, working and talking. I thought she would never let me go, but finally she gathered the cored fruit to her and padded into the kitchen.

I nearly broke my neck running to the barn. Teddy was there as he had promised.

"Now what?" I nervously asked him.

"Slip into these," he said, holding out a pair of boy's knickers and a manila-colored work shirt.

I took the clothing from him and stepped inside the barn to change. "Why in the world do you want me to wear these?"

"So you'll look like a boy," he answered matter-of-factly.

The trousers smelled as if they had lain in the bottom of a cedar trunk for a thousand years. I could hardly stand to pull them on over my stockings. Besides that, they were a very gaudy color of green. I felt like an ugly Christmas tree, the kind that no one ever picks to decorate in the parlor.

"Hurry up or we'll miss the show," Teddy called as he peeked around the corner of the barn.

I tucked an equally stinky shirt into the pants and sat down to pull on the lace-up boy's boots Teddy handed to me. Teddy stood there, watching me and smiling. When I stood up he passed me a slouch hat. It was all I could do to tuck my clean hair under the cap's rim.

"Now you need a little dirt on your face," he said as he smeared some mud on my cheeks without even asking if he could.

"Why?" I asked, brushing off a clump of the filth.

"So you'll look more like a scruffy kid instead of a girl." Teddy stepped back and smiled widely. "It's no use, Lizzie."

"What's no use?"

"No matter what, you still look beautiful." He smiled again, this time with the enthusiasm of an old maid at a barn dance.

"You know, if my brothers catch us at this, they'll kill you and make me watch."

Teddy smiled shyly. "Don't worry about it. It's worth the risk." We left the safety of the barn and sprinted toward the medicine show tents.

It didn't occur to me that I hadn't brought any ticket money until we were in front of the hurdy-gurdy. "I don't have any cash," I told Teddy.

"Me neither," he said, "but I have something better."

"What?"

"My uncle is with the show. He's their promotion man and doubles as someone to take care of the riffraff if there's any trouble. I'll find him and get some free passes."

"I'll come with you. I'd like to meet your uncle."

"No, no," Teddy said quickly. "Well, see, my uncle isn't exactly the kind of man I'd want a girl like you to meet."

I smiled at Teddy as he hurried to a tent on the far side of the wagon circle. He returned with a handful of tickets.

"Did he give you all those?" I asked in disbelief.

"Sure. My uncle said it was about time I became a man." He pulled me by my hand toward the tent.

Inside the hurdy-gurdy show it was musty-smelling, and the bench we sat on was as hard as stone. Teddy sat up tall — all excited. I tried to make myself into an invisible lump and nervously kept feeling around my cap to be sure a stray red lock didn't fall to my shoulders and betray me.

As other ticket buyers took their seats, I was shocked at the men who were there. The banker had come to watch, and you can bet his fish-mouthed wife wasn't with him. Joe Henderson who ran the general mercantile was there, too, sitting on the front row between Avery Jones, the miller, and Tom Harkins, the barkeep. Sitting beside the banker was Brother Jack, and at his side, Edman. Front row. If Mother could have seen her little darlings.

After we had been inside the tent for about ten minutes, a mustached showman walked around the walls of the room and snuffed out the coal oil lanterns that had been lighting the place. Suddenly, a note or two of music drifted through the crowd. The men became deathly still, the way they did on Sundays when Reverend Pike sermonized on gambling and drinking.

The stage curtains opened slightly, and a long, naked female leg slid through the red velvet folds. The men applauded and cheered as if they had just won a prize. Teddy's face was popping teeth like a lovesick mule.

The rest of the woman followed her leg on stage. She was heavy-set and dressed in a lacy outfit that looked as if it had been pasted on her with flour and water. She called into the crowd, "Is everybody happy?"

The men chorused, "Happy, ma'am." It was easy to tell they had been there before.

She smiled and began to dance, slowly and in rhythm to a sultry song coming from an off-tune organ Uriah Weeks was cranking beside the stage.

The men began to chatter and chuckle like old Slap Happy. They acted so much like squirrels, I thought maybe I should warn them that hunting season was coming up.

A trio of women joined the first dancing floozy on stage. Between the four of them, they had the men hopping up and down in their seats like jack-in-the-boxes. I began to feel sick, sick and disgusted, especially at my brothers' behavior. Jack was holding his fingers to his mouth and letting out train whistles, and Edman, nice, quiet Edman, was actually standing on a bench, slapping his thighs in rhythm to the women's swaying hips.

"It's time for you know who," the husky-voiced ringleader of the women teased, as she shooed the others to the back of the stage and motioned toward the curtains.

Another woman, at least six feet five, stamped across the stage. Her legs were longer than the trunk of a five-year-old elm, and she stopped her flapping boughs right in front of the banker. He nearly lost his artificial teeth.

"Who are you going to please tonight, Lucie?" the first woman asked the giant-sized woman.

"Someone new," Lucie thundered.

The men started yelling, "Me! Me! Me!"

Lucie waved her hands in the air, and the shouting stopped. She stepped down from the stage and, to the beat of the music, paraded through the crowd, touching fuzzy-faced boys, thrilling gray-bearded grandpas, and coming to stand directly by Teddy and me.

Teddy smiled up at her like a puppy about to get a bone, and I turned my face away and tugged my hat down over my eyes. The next thing I noticed was that there was a hand on my shoulder — a big, firm hand that belonged to six-feet-five legs.

"What about you, sonny?" the woman asked me.

"She . . . he doesn't feel real good," I heard Teddy sputter.

"This will make him feel all better," the woman teased. "Here, sonny, help yourself to my garter."

I peeked up long enough to see that the Lucie woman had propped her mile-long leg beside me on the bench and was pushing a black-lace garter down her exposed thigh. Over her knee I could see Jack and Edman's smiling faces.

"Should Lucie give him some help?" the woman called to the crowd.

"Get him started," a man yelled.

The woman reached down and took my hand, placing it on her thigh. I felt a million goosebumps run the length of my arm and come to settle as a lump in my throat. Then she gave me a little tap on my head and a lone, stray curl slipped out from under my cap.

It was instant exposure. I glanced across the room and saw Jack and Edman talking to each other. Edman's face was as red as a beet and Jack was already starting toward us.

"They know, Teddy," I whispered. I slid from the bench and started toward the tent opening.

Teddy yelled, "Yikes!" pushing the hurdy-gurdy woman between him and Jack's flailing fists.

I didn't stay around very long. Just long enough to glance back behind the running Teddy to see Edman and Jack both fall over Lucie, knocking her and her half-removed garter flat to the floor.

The laughter from the crowd was thunderous, but I didn't care to hear any more of it. Teddy and I ran like the Devil himself was on our tails. I could almost feel the flames of Hell lapping at my back, and an occasional imaginary poke of a pitchfork pushed me to speeds never before known to my feet.

* The Red-eyed Man *

Teddy and I hurried to Baby Ethel's tent. I called to her, and when she didn't answer we slipped inside.

"Think she will mind us being in here?" Teddy asked skeptically.

"She won't mind."

We had been there only a few minutes when Baby Ethel came inside, carrying a basket full of her dried laundry.

"Who . . . who . . . who are you?" she asked shakily. Her eyes were huge with fright.

I whipped my cap to my side and let the rest of my tattletale hair fall around my shoulders. "It's Lizzie."

After a quick glance at Teddy, Baby Ethel set down her clothes basket and asked me, "Why are you dressed like a boy?"

"Look, Ethel," I started, "it's too long a story to tell. I'll explain later. Right now, Teddy and I need somewhere to hide."

Suddenly, we could hear excited voices approaching the tent from across the show grounds. I could hear Jack talking loudly.

I whispered, "We need to hide from *them*."

As the voices got closer, Baby Ethel pointed to a large trunk beside the tent door. In a moment Teddy and I were tucked inside it, with the lid open only a crack for air.

The next sound we heard was Jack calling for Baby Ethel to let Edman and him inside her tent.

"You Baby Ethel?" Jack asked rudely when Ethel pushed back the canvas opening. From my hiding place I could see the toes of his brogans.

"Yes, I am," Ethel said sweetly. "Sorry, boys, but my booth doesn't open until later this evening."

"We didn't come to see your show," Edman explained, sounding a little embarrassed.

"Oh, then, maybe you wanted to see the bearded lady. She's in the next tent."

"No, no," Jack stuttered. "We're hunting for our sister, Lizzie Bingman. She comes down here and visits you a lot."

"Haven't seen anyone who looks like Lizzie today."

"She's dressed like a boy," Jack explained. "And she's with a no-good, yellow-bellied skunk named Teddy Hargrove."

"I'm sorry," Ethel said kindly as she moved toward the tent entrance. "But if I see Lizzie, I'll tell her you're looking for her."

"No need to do that," Jack said as his feet moved out of my sight. "She knows darn well we're after her."

As Edman followed Jack outside, he said, "She knows we'll find her, too."

When they had gone, Baby Ethel helped Teddy and

me out of the trunk. We sat on its lid for a while, thinking.

"What now, Teddy?" I finally asked. My legs were aching from the fast getaway.

"I have to get you home," he answered, mostly to himself. "Then I can take chances on my own." He looked long at me. "Is that okay with you, Lizzie?"

"Home sounds like the safest place," I agreed. "At least there I don't think either of my brothers would punch me in the nose — or worse."

Teddy peeked outside and turned back to say, "There's no one in sight. I think the best route is along the creek, down by the grape arbor."

"But the woods are so heavy between there and my house," I protested.

"We'll get to the arbor and hide out until dusk, and then you can run on home," he said matter-of-factly. He turned to Baby Ethel and said, "Thank you for your help. It saved our lives."

I gave Baby Ethel a quick hug before Teddy pulled me by my sleeve out through the medicine show tents toward our hiding place.

The grape arbor was a place I had been forbidden to go, and with good reason. Most of the bad men in town met there at least twice a week to drink and gamble and do other things I'd heard about, but couldn't imagine.

Most of the kids were interested in what went on at the arbor because of what the gamblers left behind. Mostly their trash consisted of hickory nuts they would let drop out of their pockets. The nuts were their snacks while they gambled. Sometimes, though, a kid might find a bottle half full of booze and have the privilege of finishing it. A real lucky scavenger could come up with a nickel or dime. Edman had bragged about once finding a silver dollar there.

The arbor was dark and damp. The huge grapevines were as thick as my wrists and hung in giant loops over the oak trees. They made a canopy over the lower branches of the trees, and under the limbs it was as dark as a stormy night. Usually, the men who gambled there built a small campfire at the entrance to the viney cave, but there was no campfire when Teddy and I arrived. There was only a black, forbidden-looking hole leading into the woods.

"Come on inside, there's no one here," Teddy assured me as he took hold of my hand.

I felt a chill run from my toes to my scalp, making me shiver. "It looks snaky in there," I said.

"Come on, now, Lizzie."

"No one we know would go in there."

"Your brothers would."

"I don't think so," I said, knowing full well that every single one of them *had* been in the arbor.

"They would in a minute and you know it."

I bit my trembling lip and let Teddy drag me inside the cave. I didn't even look down, but at least twice I felt something slithery brush against my foot.

We sat at the back of the cave, behind a couple of crates left there. Teddy let me lean against him. He had used his father's cologne and smelled like bay leaves.

I guess I fell asleep, because the next thing I noticed was that I felt damp, and when I opened my eyes I could see a flickering flame at the end of the cave. The smell of woodsmoke was pungent.

"Teddy, wake up," I whispered.

"I am awake," he said softly. "Sit quiet, there's some men come to gamble."

"What time is it?"

"I figure supper's on the table," he answered sullenly. "But we can't leave until they do."

When my eyes adjusted to the darkness of the arbor, I could see two figures in the fireglow. One of the men was short and fat. He talked loudly and nervously. The other man was large — tall and big-boned. His speech was rough and quick. They milled around the newly started fire for a while, then sat down beside it, pulling liquor bottles from their hip pockets.

After a few minutes, the big man took a deck of cards from his vest, and the two of them began to play. The game ended, and the short, fat man dug deep into his pocket to pay the other player. The tall man laughed hoarsely.

It didn't look as if they were planning to leave. I could imagine how worried my family probably was. And I could also imagine the scriptures I'd be memorizing for being late for supper.

Suddenly, while I was thinking about how angry Mother would be, the short man jumped up and pulled a long knife out from under his jacket.

The tall man screamed, "Why you stinking little runt!" He knocked the other man's hand aside and gave him a stiff blow to the jaw.

The shorter man fell to the ground and crawled backward across the floor before he pulled himself up with the help of the arbor wall. He was breathing loudly and mumbling curse words.

"Someone ought to teach you a lesson," the other man said. Reaching into his coat, he pulled out a short-nosed gun. "Think I'll give you something to remember me by. No one messes around with —"

Before he could finish speaking, the little man lunged at him, shouting, "You don't have the nerve!"

There was a flash of fire and an explosion. The little man was thrown against the side of the grape arbor. He hit hard and slid to the dirt.

The big man didn't seem to know what to do. First he laid the gun down. Then he picked it up and looked at it. I could hear the moans of the other man as he squirmed on the floor.

Cursing loudly, the big man unloaded three more shots into the other one even as he pleaded for his life.

After that the silence was so thick I could hear the whistle at the mines sounding "last man out," even though it was ten miles away. I wanted to scream. I felt my mouth open and the pressure of air rise from my lungs. Just as I made a tiny mewing sound, Teddy clamped his hand over my mouth.

We sat there like that, me fighting a Comanche yell and Teddy muffling it with his trembling hand, until the big man gathered the cards and the money and, with a final glance toward the man on the ground, kicked out the fire and left.

Teddy took me by the hand and led me to the entrance of the arbor. I didn't even look at the man lying by the fire. Instead, I closed my eyes and followed Teddy as if I were walking in a dream.

We padded through the leaf-carpeted woods, trying to get to the field that led to my house. I had to stop and throw up by a cedar tree. I knew Teddy was sick, too, because he was so quiet.

I wiped my mouth on my sleeve and started down the trail. I saw Teddy just ahead. He looked like a shadow tucked in among the pines. Just as I started to call out to him, I felt a jerk around my neck. A long, hairy arm held me tight. I knew it was the killer. He smelled like whiskey and smoke.

"Get over here, boy," the big man ordered Teddy.

Teddy just stood.

"Get over here," the man warned, "or I'll fix your little sweetie but good."

I wanted to tell Teddy to run on, that the man wouldn't hurt me. I didn't know whether it was the murderer's arm choking off my words, or fear hanging tight to my vocal chords, but I couldn't say a thing.

Teddy jumped, then turned and ran away from us.

The big man turned me toward him after Teddy was out of sight down the trail. He had a drooping black mustache and tiny, red-veined eyes. They were sad brown eyes caught in weblike scarlet nets. "So you saw me do something bad, huh, little missy?"

I couldn't answer.

"Didn't count on that," he said thoughtfully. "Didn't count on that at all."

I tried to scream, but he clasped a big hand over my mouth and began to drag me back toward the arbor.

"The Lord is my Shepherd, I shall not want," I began to myself. "Oh, Mother, I'm sorry for the way I've been acting. Oh, Jack, you were right. I need you now."

Outside the arbor, the man loosened his grip on my arm and uncovered my mouth. He put his revolver under my chin and said firmly, "Don't scream, or it will be the last sound you make on earth."

In my mind I could see Teddy jack-rabbiting through the fields for help. Our farm was the closest; surely he would go there. But even then it would probably be too late. They would all come to the arbor to find me bullet-riddled, lying by the dead gambler in the cave, a night bird mourning for me from the branch of a spreading oak. *Then* my brothers would be sorry for the way they had been treating me.

The sound of someone walking through the darkening woods brought me back to my senses.

"Who's out there?" the red-eyed man questioned. He cocked the gun at my neck.

A soft voice asked, "That you, J.E.?" There was a rustle in the trees and the timber echoed with night sounds.

The red-eyed man stepped around me to peer into the woods. As he moved I kicked his shin with all the strength I could summon. He let me go and began to hop around. I ran through the woods down the path I thought led home.

I lost the trail only a few minutes into the trees, but I kept running. Blackberry briars tore at my legs and low-hanging branches slapped against my face. I heard footsteps somewhere nearby in the woods. My mind ran wild with questions. Was it Teddy? Maybe Papa? Maybe the murderer? The man from the woods, maybe he would help me. Maybe the J.E. he was calling was the man who had been holding me.

I had seen a man killed, lifted up on a blanket of fire, his life snuffed out like a candle's flame. Over what? A card game? A taste of whiskey? A handful of hickory nuts?

The sound of footsteps came closer. I was out of breath. Exhausted. Sick. Scared. Finally, I stumbled down on a pile of rocks, ready to meet my end. The headlines in the *Granby Gazette* would read: ELIZABETH LEE BINGMAN FOUND DEAD IN WOODS. Only Half Mile from Parents' Farm. Wearing boy's clothing. Smelling of booze. Hurdy-gurdy tickets found in her pocket. Shamed her family. Her name stricken from the family Bible. Buried in potter's field. Forever doomed and damned.

I stopped writing my obituary long enough to look up from my perch. In front of me was a pair of trousers, the legs spread wide in a defiant stance. I didn't dare look up to see who it was. I just covered my eyes and held my breath. "Ashes to ashes and dust to dust," I whispered, expecting the next time I saw daylight to be at the Pearly Gates, with Saint Peter giving me a stiff lecture on equality.

* The Medicine Show *

A hand grabbed my arm and pulled me up as if I were a fish on a line. The hand was Jack's. His mouth was drawn taut and he looked as if he could spit nails.

"Where have you been hiding all afternoon?" he yelled.

I whispered, "Please, Jack, please. Let's get out of here, and I'll explain everything."

"You can bet you're going to explain everything," he said as he yanked me along behind him. It felt as if my feet touched the ground only twice between the woods and our barn.

Jack led me into the barn and lit a lamp in a horse stall.

"You won't believe it. You just won't believe what I saw," I breathed.

"Try me," he said snottily as he drew a keg up against the door and sat down. "I believe you could do anything."

"Teddy and I hid at the arbor."

Jack looked smug. "I'll beat him to a pulp."

"While we were there we saw a man murdered."

Jack tipped back the keg he was sitting on and asked, "You expect me to believe that? I wasn't born yesterday."

"It's the truth, so help me John Brown!"

"Who was killed?"

"I didn't see his face."

"Who killed him?"

"I hadn't seen the man before."

"You say Hargrove saw all this, too?"

"He saw."

Jack sat and thought for a moment.

When he didn't speak, I asked, "Should I tell Papa and have him send for the sheriff?"

Jack didn't say anything.

"A man's dead. As lifeless as a stone. Find Teddy and ask him about it."

"You're *not* going to tell Papa," Jack said with surety. "You're not going to tell anyone about this. I wouldn't put it past Hargrove to have staged the whole thing so you could fall into his hero arms. You could make a blamed fool of yourself and your family if you tell a story like that and there's not a lick of truth to it." He stood up, got a sack from beside the keg, and handed it to me.

"What's this?" When he didn't answer I peeked inside and saw my everyday clothing. "Why did you bring these out here?"

"So you can get dressed and not go into the house looking like an urchin." He motioned toward the clothes. "Edman and I told Mother you spent the afternoon with Betsy Davis. That's what you'll tell her, too."

"That's an out and out lie, Jack."

"You're not going into the house and tell Mother you spent the afternoon at a hurdy-gurdy and in the grape arbor with Teddy Hargrove."

"But a man was murdered."

"That's what you say."

"You mean, you don't believe me, Jack?" Tears filled my eyes.

"Get dressed. I'll talk to Hargrove tomorrow. Keep your mouth shut until then."

"Just tell me that you believe me, Jack. I need for you to believe me," I pleaded.

He whirled toward me. "Thought you didn't need anyone, Lizzie!"

Jack stomped toward the house and didn't hear me whisper, "I was wrong." I would give him until tomorrow to talk to Teddy. I felt I owed him that for saving my life.

Mother didn't doubt the story about my being at Betsy's that afternoon. Jack and Edman had done a good job of lying to her. She even set me a plate for a late supper and afterward kissed me lightly on the cheek as she wished me a good night.

But it wasn't a good night. I dreamed the murder scene over and over. The red-eyed man kept getting bigger and bigger until he was the size of a giant, and it was me he was firing the bullets into. Every time one of the imaginary shots hit me, I'd jump in bed. By morning I was a wreck. When I went downstairs to breakfast, Aunt Mittie said I looked like death warmed over.

I also started to cough, probably the gift of the damp
arbor. By lunchtime, I was a hacking invalid. I forgot my
sickness for a while when Jack came back from town. I
knew he had gone to talk to Teddy.

"Well? What did Teddy say?" I asked Jack when I
found him washing his hands at the pump.

Jack rubbed lather up his arms and rinsed them under
the cool water before he said, "Look, Lizzie, I know
you've been acting . . . strange . . . all summer . . ."

"Did you talk to Teddy?" I asked impatiently.

Jack looked into my eyes. "Hargrove says he didn't
see any such thing as a murder," he explained slowly.
"He says you fell asleep. Maybe you dreamed it."

"I'll tell Papa. The sheriff should go get the body," I
said.

"I checked at the arbor. There is no body," Jack said
softly.

"No body?"

"And no talk of a murder in town."

"There was someone else in the woods besides the
murderer. Maybe he helped him carry the body
away . . ."

Jack patted me on the shoulder as if I was good dog
Shep. "Now, now, Lizzie."

"Get your grimy mitts off me!" I yelled. "I never
thought I'd live to see the day you wouldn't believe a
word I said." I ran into the house and upstairs to my
bedroom. I paced, trying to think of a reason Teddy
might have to lie about seeing the murder. Maybe the
red-eyed man had found him and threatened his life.
Maybe he was after both of us. I knew I should have told

Papa, but maybe Jack was right — I could have dreamed it all.

I felt my neck. It still hurt where the murderer had grabbed me. You don't get bruises in a dream. I threw myself across my bed and cried for hours. When I went down to supper, I looked like a washed-out prune.

At breakfast the next day, George and Edman were beside themselves with excitement. The train carrying the rest of the Longman Circus and Medicine Show had arrived at the depot. They knew most of the other boys they ran around with were already there, helping to unload crates packed with the concessions and circus equipment.

There were also the animals to watch being unloaded. First out would be the stars of the Dog and Pony Show — there were at least a hundred in the cast. They would be followed by the elephants and caged lions and monkeys.

The boys crammed their oatmeal into their mouths and ran from the table, mumbling, "Excuse me, ma'am," to Mother. I knew they would spit out their cheekloads under the lilac bush beside the front gate.

Mother and I were left alone in the kitchen. I was going to tell her about what I had seen at the grape arbor, but before I could start she looked fondly at me and said, "Lizzie, you have been behaving yourself lately. For being such a lady, here is a token of my appreciation." She held a tiny, beaded purse toward me.

With great guilt, I took the gift and stroked its fine handiwork.

"Look inside," Mother said, smiling.

I unfastened its clasp and saw a crisp five-dollar bill tucked inside. "For me?" I asked.

"For the circus," Mother explained. "I know your papa never gives you enough . . ." She stopped talking and shook her head as she stood up to clear the table.

"Mother, I don't deserve —"

"Take it, and if you feel you must do something for it, keep your eye on George today while you're in town," she said sweetly as she set an armload of plates on the cabinet and walked over to me to place a kiss on the top of my head.

Again, I started to tell Mother about what I had seen, but Hanna flew in from the parlor, dressed for sightseeing and jabbering like one of the circus monkeys. I excused myself to the back porch. Unfortunately, Hanna followed me outside and came to stand smack in front of me.

"What do you want?" I asked her when I noticed a sly smile creeping across her face.

"Oh, nothing," she answered in a singsong as she reached over and snatched the new purse from my hands. "Aunt Lana bought *you* this and for what? Visiting a seedy show and lounging away your afternoon in the arms of Teddy Hargrove?"

"How did you know?" I asked, amazed.

"I have my ways," Hanna teased. "Why, you were the hit of the hurdy-gurdy from what I heard."

"I suppose you're going to tell Mother."

"What? And break her proper little heart?" Hanna

started to laugh. She bobbed and bounced her fuzzy blond head.

"I suppose your silence has a price?"

"I'll start with this purse."

Quickly, I took it back and managed to slip the five-dollar bill from its fold before she reached for it again. As she took hold of the purse with her left hand, she brought her right hand up into the air and slapped me hard on the cheek.

I doubled up my fists and was about to let Hanna have a mouthful of knuckles, but Aunt Mittie came to the back door and asked shrilly, "Has either of you girls seen Santee?"

I turned my reddened cheek away from her and answered, "No, ma'am."

Hanna put on an innocent face and said sweetly, "Maybe he's in the parlor. I saw his cage door open this morning."

Aunt Mittie hurried away, muttering, "Oh, dear."

I stepped toward Hanna, but she backed away and said, "Temper, temper, now, Cousin Lizzie. You so much as breathe heavily on me and I'll spill all."

I could tell by her smart-alecky look that she would, and backed away to lean against the porch railing. As she started inside, I asked, "What have I ever done to you, Hanna, to deserve to be treated like this?"

"Why, Cousin Lizzie, you're upsetting the apple cart." She walked back to me and glared at me with her slimy-looking blue eyes.

"What 'apple cart'?"

"That's just an expression. You are disturbing things

as they are. You, and others like you, are trying to ruin things for the rest of us."

"Who're the 'rest of us'?"

"The other girls."

"What *other girls?*"

"All of womankind," Hanna answered dramatically, clutching the stolen purse to her heart. I thought she was going to swoon.

I could only stare at her chalk-white face.

She preached, "You think it's easy going around like this in the blazing summer heat?" She pulled at her ruffled pinafore and rustled her long, full skirt.

"You could wear one less petticoat," I suggested. She started to steam, so I added, "Or give up your lace bloomers."

"Leave it to you to say something like that," Hanna squealed. "Women are supposed to dress this way. It pleases the men. There are rules to the game, Lizzie."

"What game?" I asked Hanna's reddening face.

"The game of *life.*"

"I missed out on the rules."

"Eden," she breathed. "It started with Eve in Eden." It seemed as if I had heard that story before.

"Eve was as naked as a jaybird," I reminded her.

"She sinned and got this burden."

"What burden?"

"Petticoats," Hanna snapped.

A sudden vision of Eve walking in the cool of the evening with God, telling him the Devil had slithered up to her and talked her into wearing petticoats set off my funny bone.

"It's nothing to laugh about," Hanna lectured. "Women got demoted to second place, and that's where we're doomed to stay."

"I don't believe God had that in mind," I said. "He sent Jesus. And Jesus had plenty of women friends."

"Don't you dare blaspheme!" Hanna said piously. "You had better see the light before you walk down that road of despair."

"Thank you for the warning, Reverend Hanna." I wondered if she was going to sing a hymn and take an offering.

"Your day of reckoning is coming," she warned as she hurried toward the back door. I prayed she would trip on her halo.

The minute I got to the crowded downtown, I knew it would be hard to keep up with George. The only excitement he got on regular days was hurrying down to the mercantile to watch the banana stalks from South America being unpacked. Occasionally, a tarantula made the trip packed in with the fruit. Every boy in town wanted one of the woolly spiders. George had got one once and had hung it on a string and tried to scare me with it. He learned his lesson about startling me when I picked up a hammer and bashed his grizzly pet on the head.

I found George and Edman standing on the dock at the depot. They were watching the last of the elephants being led away. George was covered with something brown and smelled like peanuts. I figured he had attacked a candy bar. Edman was battling a large paper cone topped with floss candy. He spent what time he wasn't eating wiping the sticky stuff off of his spectacles.

"I'm supposed to keep an eye on you," I told George.

"Which eye, Lizzie?" George asked, smiling at me with chocolate-covered teeth. "The one in your potato head or the one in your needle-sized brain?"

I would have taken the time to shove his face in a water trough, but I saw Baby Ethel peek out of her tent. I left the goon brothers on their own and hurried over to her.

Baby Ethel opened the tent flap and asked, "Did everything work out all right yesterday?"

"Ethel, I need to talk," I said as I hurried her inside the tent.

Baby Ethel sat down on a trunk. "What is it, Lizzie? You look as if you've seen a ghost."

"I'm afraid I *might* have." I sat down beside her and took her hands into mine. "I need for you to believe me."

"I'll try."

"When Teddy and I left here yesterday, we went to a place called the grape arbor. While we were hiding we saw a man *murdered*."

Baby Ethel gasped and pulled her hands away to put them over her mouth.

"He was killed in cold blood right in front of us."

Baby Ethel shook her head slowly. "You poor dear. And now you're afraid he's after you."

"He could be."

"Didn't the sheriff arrange for some protection?"

I stood up. "I didn't go to the sheriff."

"Then your father will look after you," Baby Ethel said.

I turned toward the canvas flap. "I didn't tell him either."

"Who *did* you tell?"

"My brother Jack."

"And?"

"And he checked things out and found there had been no murder, at least according to Teddy."

Baby Ethel said, "Oh dear, oh dear. What are you going to do?"

"I honestly don't know. There's no body. No proof. Just the word of a girl who was caught in a hurdy-gurdy."

"I wish I could help you," Baby Ethel said. "I won't even be here after this afternoon to comfort you."

I glanced around the tent and saw that Baby Ethel had been packing her clothes. "Are you leaving so soon?"

"Yes," she answered wearily. "Remember, when the circus gets to town, we move on. The last performance of the medicine show is at four o'clock, then we take to the road."

"What am I going to do, Ethel?"

She tipped her head as if she was trying very hard to think of something. "I know," she finally suggested. "You find Teddy and ask him why he denied the murder. Seems without him you don't have a chance."

I gave Baby Ethel a quick hug. "You're absolutely right. I'll talk to Teddy, then I'll tell Papa."

"If you can, let me know what happens before we leave town," Baby Ethel said as I hurried outside.

I turned back and waved to her. It was nice to have a real friend.

I spent most of the morning following George and Edman. Lucky for me they ran out of money by noon and decided to spend the rest of the day at the tent where the ladies of the local churches served lunch. Mother was there, dishing up cole slaw and baked beans, so she agreed to look after them.

My throat had started to hurt from the cold I'd caught. The coughing was getting louder, too. I knew if Mother heard me hacking she would send me home, and I hadn't seen Teddy yet, so I slipped away.

I hurried to the last performance of the medicine show. When I got there a man who called himself Uncle Ben was standing on a stage fastened to the back of one of the wagons. He was holding a bottle of red-colored medicine in his hand. "It'll cure all your ills, all your ailments — the rheumatiz, the consumption, parasites, pleurisy, all the infirmities that plague mortal man," he chanted.

A man behind Uncle Ben slapped a fiddle against his chin and began to make the catgut squawk. A woman with a tambourine joined him and began to beat out a raspy rhythm. To the music and Uncle Ben's pleading, people began to pass money into the barker's hands, returning to their places in the crowd with bottles of the miracle drug clutched to their chests and contented looks on their faces.

I saw Aunt Mittie in the crowd. She grabbed at a catch

in her hip and made her way to the front row to purchase a bottle of the remedy. She hurried back to stand by her beau and slipped the medicine into her handbag. If Mother knew Aunt Mittie had once again given away hard cash for a promise, she would have lectured her for all she was worth.

About halfway through the program, I saw Jack coming toward me. He dragged me away from the medicine show stage and said, "You shouldn't be standing around without an escort in front of a man who sells that kind of stuff. It would drug a horse."

"Leave me alone," I said wearily. I moved closer to the wagon so I could hear how Uncle Ben's remedy would make me more healthy, vivacious, and beautiful.

"Go help Mother at the church tent," Jack insisted as he dragged me away again.

"Mother doesn't need me," I protested.

"Look, all the other *decent* women are over there, doing their share for the community," Jack lectured.

"Aunt Mittie is here," I informed him. "Besides, I'm not decent, remember? I'm the hurdy-gurdy girl. I'm the girl you won't even believe when she says she saw a murder."

Jack steamed, mumbling, "I'll let that go because I think you are losing your mind, but just keep it up . . ."

"Oh, stop it, Jack. Wait until you and Rosie are married and you can have your own little girl to boss around. I certainly don't need another parent."

"I'd sure treat you differently than Mother and Papa do. I'd cut me a switch and wear you out," he bellowed. "You're acting like trash. Doing things you shouldn't be doing in the name of . . . equality. You don't want *equality*, Lizzie. You want *exemption*. You don't want to be equal in the eyes of the law. You want to be *above* the law."

"This isn't an oration contest," I spat into his puffy red face.

"I don't want an audience," Jack ranted. "I just want you to listen to me. I'm afraid you've already gotten yourself into more trouble than you can handle. What with running around with Teddy Hargrove —"

"There's nothing wrong with Teddy."

"He's a liar. He has to be if you're telling the truth about what you saw at the grape arbor," he said snidely.

"Maybe he's scared."

"Maybe he's just like the rest of his family. Crooks and cheats."

"His father is a businessman."

"His father is a no-good. Ask anyone."

"You're just saying that."

Jack backed off. "I'm going to find Hargrove and bring him here even if I have to carry him over my shoulder. We are getting this thing settled once and for all. If he's lying and there really was a murder, all of us are in trouble for not going to the sheriff. And, sister, if you are lying, I may take a switch to you even though I am not your papa, heaven forbid!"

I stood beside Uncle Ben's wagon and listened to the rest of the performance. My throat hurt so badly I bought a bottle of the medicine, hoping for an instant cure. I intended to have a drink, then find the elusive Teddy.

I leaned against a wagon wheel and crammed the

change from my five-dollar bill into my camisole before I opened the bottle of tonic. I took a long, slow drink. The first sip of the medicine tasted good — something like the cherry cough syrup Mother ordered from the Five Drops Company.

The next swallow I took was bigger than the first, and it burned my mouth a bit, but suddenly, as Uncle Ben had promised, my throat felt better. Before I knew it, I had drunk half the bottle of medicine, and I couldn't remember having ever felt so good. I glanced through the crowd and saw Jack running toward me.

"Oh, no," I said to myself. I felt real sleepy and didn't have enough energy to go another round with Jack. I crawled into the wagon I had been standing beside.

There was a cot with a quilt spread over it inside the wagon. And just like in "Goldilocks and the Three Bears," I lay down on the little bed that was just right and pulled the covers up to my chin. Somewhere outside I could hear Jack running between the wagons, yelling, "Lizzie! Lizzie! Lizzie Bingman, where are you? I have something to tell you."

I tried to call out to him, but the only words I whispered were, "Good night, Jack," as I tucked my bottle of Uncle Ben's Remedy in beside me and drifted away on a red-cherry cloud.

❋ The Poster Man ❋

A hot, chafing wind blew over me. I reached up and clumsily brushed my hair away from my eyes, and turned to my side to kick my feet free of the bed covers. The sheets on the ticking smelled musty. Mother must have been out of borax when she did the laundry.

I opened my eyes to peek at the sun and see what time it was, but when I finally managed to focus on where the window in my bedroom should have been, I remembered where I was. In the back of a wagon. I glanced above me and the rumpled canvas ceiling told me I had put the puzzle together correctly.

When I sat up and smoothed my dress, I heard voices outside the wagon. They were accompanied by the low rumble of threatening thunder.

"Guess we'll move on after breakfast," one deep-throated voice said.

"Made good time last night, good time. But need to be on our way," another voice agreed.

"Last night," I said to the cot. "How long have I been here?" I stood up quickly, but plopped back onto the bed when the wagon opening spun. My head felt as if someone had stepped on it.

When I finally managed to climb out of the wagon, I could see we weren't in Granby. From the way the wind was whipping through a sparsely populated grove of cottonwoods beside the circle of wagons, I wondered if we were even in Missouri.

"Who's this?" a man across the campsite asked as he walked toward me.

I slowly answered, "I'm Lizzie Bingman."

"Get Marlin," the man ordered a skinny kid who had run up to stand beside me. "Appears we have a stowaway."

I smiled and said, "I guess I fell asleep in one of your wagons."

"Always wanted to join the circus, huh, honey?" he asked laughing.

"It was the Uncle Ben's Remedy I drank."

He nodded knowingly and led me to a place beside a campfire. A fat woman with dangling ear bobs handed me a cup of thick coffee. I took a sip of the brew and tried not to spit it into the coals. From the looks on the faces of the medicine show people, I began to feel as if I'd been shanghaied into their traveling family. I felt my stomach flip-flop. To my great relief, Baby Ethel appeared in the crowd and rushed over to me, asking shrilly, "Lizzie Bingman, what are you doing here? My word! My word!"

"I went to sleep in the back of a wagon," I told her.

"We're in *Kansas*," Baby Ethel declared. "Crossed the border last night."

"I have to get home," I said, suddenly realizing that probably everyone and his dog was out searching for me. "My family will be worried sick."

Baby Ethel looked at the crowd, focusing on a big man dressed in gray-striped trousers and a dingy-looking silk shirt. She asked, "Think you could take her back, Marlin?"

The man pulled on the cuffs of his shirt and answered, "Don't much see how I can do that until tomorrow. If Jake gets back tonight, maybe he can take her home."

Baby Ethel turned toward me. "Guess that's the best we can do, Lizzie. You'll have to wait until Jake can take you back."

I nodded and finished drinking the bitter coffee.

Jake, their poster man, didn't catch up with the moving wagons at noon as he was supposed to. He still wasn't there when they circled the wagons to make camp for the night. I began to get scared. The Gypsy women cooking supper around the glowing campfire looked like dancing shadows. Their teeth were too white, and their constant laughter seemed sinister.

I noticed Lucie from the hurdy-gurdy among them. I thought she didn't recognize me, but before I followed Ethel to her wagon for the night, she passed by me and asked, "Been offered any garters lately?" She laughed as she said, "That little fall jarred my foundation."

"Sorry, ma'am," I managed to say as she walked away.

Baby Ethel and I shared a supper of beans and hush puppies in her wagon. "Got to be in Dodge City before the big fair opens there in about a week," she explained as she spread a quilt on the floor.

I got up from the trunk where I had been sitting and started to lie down on the pallet she had made.

"No! No!" Baby Ethel cried. "Lizzie, the cot's for you." Her bed was a large mattress laid over three pieces of thick timber.

"I couldn't," I protested, quickly sitting down on the wagon floor.

"You're my guest." She reached out to pull me up beside her. "I want you to take my bed."

"I couldn't. I mean it."

She looked as if I'd slapped her.

"What if both of us slept on the bed," I suggested. "There seems to be plenty of room."

Baby Ethel pulled back the covers and smiled as we crawled into the bed. We pulled the sheet over us and held hands as we lay in the dark. I rolled toward her only after I heard her breathing drop into the slow humdrum of sleep. I laid my head on her limp nightgown and felt sorry that she didn't have a mother to starch her bedclothing.

I began to think about Mother, and the more I thought about her, the more miserable I felt. Hanna had probably told her everything by now. Mother would be at home, lying across her feather bed and crying into her pillow for me. I was so lonely for Mother I would have given anything to hear her voice, even if she was assigning me the whole Bible to memorize.

Before daylight, Baby Ethel awakened me. "Jake's

here," she said. "He'll be needing to get you back to Granby as soon as he can."

"Now?" I asked sleepily.

"Come on, Lizzie. Jake's an impatient man. If you want to get home, hurry up and wash your face for the trip," she insisted.

I slipped from the cot and quickly ran a damp cloth over my face. I brushed my hair back with my hands and tidied my dress. Baby Ethel went outside to get some food for me to take on the trip. I met her where the horses were tethered and she showed me to a short-legged mule I was to mount because Jake was on his way.

I placed the parcel Ethel had fixed for me on my lap and let the mule follow Jake's big bay gelding into a strip of woods. The man was dressed in a rain slicker and he had a shabby hat pulled down over his face.

I reined my mule around to yell a final word to Baby Ethel. When I did, Jake turned his horse and rode up beside me, acting annoyed.

"Good-bye, Ethel," I called through the trees.

"Good-bye, Lizzie," she answered faintly. "Hope to see you again, real soon."

Before I could answer, Jake pulled the reins of my mule and turned the animal around so I was facing him. In the first light of the cloudy morning I saw his face. Sitting atop his lip was a long, dark mustache.

"Answer her. Make it real smart," the red-eyed man ordered, patting his coat pocket.

I caught my breath.

"Answer her," he demanded. He reached over and grabbed my arm.

"Guess I'll see you next year when the medicine show comes to town," I called to Baby Ethel. "Maybe my *sisters* won't be as much trouble as they have been this year."

Baby Ethel waved slowly, then dropped her hand to her side and stared at me, speechless.

I looked into Jake's face and tried not to faint. He led my mule across the prairie. The only sound I heard, other than the clopping of our mounts' hooves against the soggy field grasses, was the beating of my heart, like a smithy's hammer on a horseshoe. The only hope I had was if Baby Ethel remembered I only had brothers. I hoped she would remember in time.

We rode along for a couple of hours. I felt like a lamb being led to slaughter as Jake bent over his saddle, pulling me along with slow determination, probably picking a nice sandy place to dig a grave. I had a feeling there was a spade in his gear — one freshly caked with river-bottom mud. And I knew somewhere in his pockets was a short-nosed revolver that spoke a clear, loud message.

If he buried me in Kansas, I knew Mother would never get over it. She had always said the only things in Kansas were grasshoppers six inches long, cockleburs, and Jay Hawkers, and that those were the niceties. Now she could add to her list one lost and sorry Missouri girl. Even in death, I wouldn't be able to please her.

By mid-morning the clouds had cleared away and the huge, bloody-red sun had settled in to steam the soggy prairie. Jake reined his horse to a stop at a stand of shrubbery beside a tiny stream.

"Get down," he ordered, motioning toward a rock beside the bubbling water.

I got off my mule and sat on the rock. He handed me a strip of jerky and a cup of water. At least I wouldn't go to the grave hungry. I ate slowly, watching Jake down his meal like a hungry dog attacking a pork chop.

We rested at the stream for over an hour. Jake spent his time walking the bank and looking beyond the bushes to a visible strip of prairie. Just after he packed up and told me to mount again, he let out a "Yahoo" and ran toward the clearing.

I heard the sound of approaching horse hooves and thought maybe it was the second man I'd heard at the grape arbor, but when Jake led the visitor's horse to the campsite, the rider was definitely not a man.

"Howdy, girl," the newly arrived woman said, friendly like, after she had dismounted and walked over to me. She was dressed in gray riding britches and short black boots.

"Fine as can be expected, ma'am," I answered, turning away from her and hoping she wouldn't recognize me.

"You're the girl who visited the saloon," she said slowly. "Why, yes, you're that little girl who came in with her brother. Don't you remember me, girl?"

I nodded. "Your name's Dixie, ma'am."

"That's right," she said. "And you're who now?"

"Lizzie Bingman."

"From Granby," the woman said, scratching her head. "Why, Jake, I know this girl. Such a small world."

"That's too bad," he said coldly as he got the woman a piece of jerky from his saddlebag.

Dixie stared at him as she took the food, asking, "Why's she along?"

The red-eyed man patted his coat pocket and said, "She and I have some unfinished business to tend to."

I felt my stomach drop into my shoes.

"What's going on, Jake?" Dixie asked. She didn't sound afraid of him, but more like she was his mother giving him a scolding.

"It was nothing," he protested.

"He killed a man," my stupid mouth said.

"Jake, that true?" the woman asked quickly.

"It was an accident," he said. "A little cheat pulled a knife on me, and I lost my head . . ."

"Your temper, your temper," Dixie moaned. "I knew this was bound to happen." She glanced at me. "What did the girl do?"

"Saw it all," he answered plainly.

Dixie nodded to him, then turned toward me with a strange, yet patient look in her eyes. She didn't say anything more while Jake broke camp and prepared to ride.

In late afternoon we came to a roaring river. The woods around it were deep and dark, and the land lay hilly beyond it. I began to feel as if I were home in Missouri.

At least there would be friendly soil turned over me.

I began to think about Mother again. She was probably still crying, worrying about me — lost, and her men out searching the timber for her darling daughter. She was probably fretting over whether or not they would find my body. She had probably even hurried to Spencer's to make the final arrangements and select a casket.

When they brought me home, carried in Papa's arms, she would run from the front porch, dabbing at her eyes with a tiny handkerchief and moan, "My daughter. My Lizzie. My Lizzie." I could almost hear her sobbing.

I stopped thinking about home when Jake took hold of the reins on my mule and led me away from Dixie.

"Where are you taking me?" I asked shakily.

"Where do you think?" he said.

I thought about jumping down and running away, but the thought of being alone in the woods scared me about as much as being led to my grave. I'd heard tales about people lost in the timber for days, digging holes in the ground for water like dogs and running naked among the trees, not letting a soul come near them.

Jake said, "Get down off your mule, girl," as he reined his horse to a stop. He dismounted and tied the animal to a tree.

I dropped to the ground and walked with him toward the churning water.

"Stand right over there — on that rock," he ordered.

I did as I was told and stood on the rock, feeling like the target at the shooting gallery. The one where Teddy won me the Kewpie doll. Teddy? Where in the world was he, and why had he lied?

"Turn around, girl," the man ordered.

I looked across the water and sang to myself, "My home is over Jordan." I suddenly felt very religious.

At the same time that I heard the gun cocked, I heard Dixie call, "Jake, don't *shoot* her. For heaven's sake, don't put a bullet in that girl."

He yelled, "Gotta kill her. She saw me."

"Don't *shoot* her," she said, reining her horse up beside him.

"What do you want me to do, tickle her to death?"

"Just shove her into the water. Chances are she'll drown."

I thought, Thanks, but no thanks. I felt lightheaded.

"Why should I do that?" the man asked.

"Then people would think she wandered away and drowned," Dixie explained. "No use having two murders on your head."

Jake yanked me around. There was something in his eyes that said he was really going to do it. He had acted the same way at the grape arbor before he murdered the man, first toying with the idea and then carrying out the execution with an explosion of rage.

"Please, please, don't hurt me," I said in a weak voice. There was no adventure left in me as I stood there with tears streaming down my face.

He grabbed me by my hair and spun me around again. The next thing I knew I felt a hard blow to the back of my head and I toppled off the rock into the water. I went under for a minute, then bobbed to the surface. I was rapidly carried downstream, out of their sight. I tried to swim, but I could barely keep afloat and couldn't begin to paddle toward shore. So I rode the current, letting it carry me away.

In my mind I could hear Jack saying, "Now just relax, Lizzie. Don't fight the water, you'll learn to swim." It couldn't have been that many summers ago that he taught me. I would have given anything to hug his neck and feel his strong arms helping me to shore.

I hit a large rock protruding from the river bottom, and it tore off my shoes. At least after that, I could kick more easily. After fighting the current for what seemed like an eternity, I could hear a roaring sound coming from downstream. It sounded like the machinery working in the mines.

Ahead of me, not twenty feet away, was the top of what I was sure was a waterfall. I had no idea how long the fall was, but the sound of water falling was deafening.

There was little to grab between me and the plunge, except for a splattering of driftwood wedged between a couple of rocks. I thought if I hadn't been so burdened with my petticoats and bloomers, I would be light enough to swim to it, but my clothing kept me from kicking freely.

As I got to the branches, I tried to touch one of them, but I floated between the rocks, my hands never reaching the wood. Suddenly I was jerked back. I was caught on the branches — by my bloomers. Held by my drawers. Hanna would have loved it. It would make the *Granby Gazette:* LOCAL GIRL SAVED FROM DROWNING BY BLOOMERS. I could already feel my face turning red.

I rolled over and sat up in the water. I used my legs as holding places and finally got a grasp on the sticks and rocks. After I was grounded on the driftwood pile, it was simple to get to land. I just stepped along the stones and caught a piece of vine near shore, then swung to the bank. I felt like my own heroine. Maybe someone would award me a medal of courage. That is, if I were ever allowed off the front porch again. I had a gut feeling that Mother was going to see to it I memorized the entire New Testament.

From where the sun sat, I knew Jake had brought me back east a way. He had probably circled the medicine show wagons to get close to Joplin and pick up Dixie. If I kept to the stream and walked south, I knew I was headed toward home.

I made sure I left a visible trail, breaking away branches and stamping tracks in the river mud. It was almost dark when I decided to rest for the night. I was so cold that my teeth were chattering and giant-sized goose bumps were climbing my arms.

I found a place to sleep between a couple of big trees and snuggled down into the fallen leaves. A lone evening star was the last thing I saw before I closed my eyes.

A screaming crane woke me in the morning. It was dipping into the river, snapping at fish. Finally, it caught one and flapped across the water into a stand of trees.

I sat up and rubbed my feet. My stockings were in shreds, and I had a few cuts on my soles, but as Aunt Mittie would say, "Nothing a little poultice and some rest wouldn't cure." I would have given a pig a kiss for a drink from my bottle of Uncle Ben's Remedy.

Before I even had a chance to wash my face, I heard the sound of horses approaching. "It's them," I said aloud. "They saw I didn't drown."

I hurried to the creek bank and hid among the weeds there. Over the rushing water I heard, "Lizzie. Lizzie, can you hear me?"

The voice sounded like Papa's, but then Jake had a deep voice too, and knew my name.

"Lizzie, it's Jack," I heard someone call.

"Do you hear me, Lizzie? It's Papa," a rough-sounding voice called.

It *was* Papa. I knew it was by the way he called my name through his beard. I reached up and wiped away the tears that were flowing down my cheeks. I managed to yell, "Over here. I'm over here."

I saw horses as I struggled up the creek bank. Standing beside them were Papa and Jack and Edman and a couple of men from town. There was another rider with them I didn't recognize at first — not until she pulled off her hat and got down from the sorrel mare she had been riding. It was Mother. I'd never seen her sit astraddle on a horse. She was wearing riding britches and carrying a short-nosed quirt. Never before had I seen her in trousers or out in the sun without her parasol.

Mother raced to me, beating even Papa to my side. She quickly pulled me to her and hugged me hard against her chest. I thought she was going to pop me in two. "Are you all right, Elizabeth?"

I managed to take a breath and nod that I was.

"Then let's go home," she said.

Papa interrupted, "Maybe we should set up camp

and have some breakfast. Lizzie looks as if she needs rest —"

"She's able to ride," Mother insisted.

"Well, all right, all right," Papa muttered. "I'll put her on with Jack."

"She'll ride with me," Mother said firmly. "Come on, Lizzie." She pulled me along with her. I gave Papa a questioning look while Mother took to the saddle, but he just shrugged and went to his horse.

Mother looked down at me and kicked her boot free of the stirrup. "Get on up," she ordered.

I put my foot into the leather stirrup and held on to Mother's hand, letting her pull me up behind her. I wrapped my arms around her waist as she reined her horse after Papa and the others. She felt firm and lean. It shocked me that she felt that way. I'd always likened her to a fat barnyard hen or an overripe watermelon.

❋ Teddy ❋

We arrived in Granby very late that evening. Mother let me go to bed as soon as we got home, and I didn't even take off my ragged clothes before I fell across my bed in deep sleep. I dreamed I was lost in a long, dark, damp cave.

I awakened to the sounds of chickadees and meadowlarks calling from the hayfield, and the sweet, smoky scent of bacon frying. I peeled away my dirty clothes, pulled on my dressing gown, and hurried to the kitchen. It was mid-morning. I could tell because the breakfast dishes had already been cleared except for my plate.

Aunt Mittie was standing by the stove. She rushed to me and hugged me. "You nearly did it this time, didn't you, young lady?" she half-asked, half-lectured.

"Seems that way," I agreed.

She guided me toward a chair at the table and, after I was seated, served me bacon and eggs and cool, sweet cider.

"Where're Mother and Papa?" I asked through bites of breakfast.

"In the parlor, talking with Sheriff Benson."

I only nodded and continued to eat. In a moment the back door flew open and George stomped into the kitchen. He marched over to stand beside me. His fat little fingers drummed a rhythm on the oilcloth beside my plate.

"Something on your mind?" I asked him.

"You are the most hated kid in all of Granby," he answered dramatically.

"George, shut your mouth," Aunt Mittie ordered.

"No, wait, George. Tell me why I'm 'the most hated kid.' "

"The *circus*," he answered stiffly.

I laid down my fork. "What about the circus?"

"It's leaving town. Leaving for good. No monkeys, no elephants, no acrobats. Nothing. Less than nothing. And all because of you."

Aunt Mittie swung a spatula at George's behind, and he yelled when the wooden spoon made contact with his knickers. "Now get on out of here and don't speak to your sister that way," Aunt Mittie said as she opened the screen door for George's dramatic exit.

When George was yowling in the backyard I asked Aunt Mittie, "Is it because of their poster man?"

"Sheriff has him in jail," she answered.

"Did they find a body?"

Aunt Mittie sighed. "Maybe you'd better wait and talk to your papa and mother."

Aunt Mittie heated water in the cast-iron pots on the back of the stove and poured me a bath in the little room beside the kitchen. I had barely time to wash off and dry my hair before Mother and Papa were in the kitchen asking where I was.

When I was dressed, I sat at the kitchen table with them. Mother served us all coffee and then sat down beside Papa. They looked like Sitting Bull and his little sister. Before they could speak I offered, "I'm sorry."

"There's time for that later," Mother said flatly. "We have other matters to attend to now."

I looked at Papa.

He cleared his throat and said, "Lizzie, Jack told us about the murder. The posse searched the riverbank, and, indeed, a body was found. The man shot was Helliot Jones."

"The peddler?" I asked.

Papa nodded.

I remembered Mr. Jones then because he came to the farm a few times to sharpen our knives and scissors.

"And from what George says, the sheriff caught the murderer?" I asked hopefully.

"The man who was bringing you from the medicine show back to Granby is in jail," Papa said slowly.

"He's the murderer," I said excitedly.

"He says he wasn't near Granby that evening," Mother added.

"He tried to kill me out on the trail. He hit me in the back of the head and knocked me into the river," I argued, rubbing the bump his revolver butt had made.

"Lizzie, it's your word against his. And he has that woman with him who swears he was with her the night of the murder," Papa said with a consoling voice.

"It isn't just my word against that man's. Teddy saw

the murder, too. He was right there with me. He saw
Jake shoot Helliot Jones. He saw Jake catch me. Teddy
saw it *all!*" I nearly screamed.

Mother and Papa glanced at each other.

"I'm not crazy. Don't treat me as if I don't know what
I'm talking about. I know what I saw. Ask Teddy. Ask
him about the red-eyed man — Jake. Who is he,
anyway?"

Mother reached across the table and took hold of my
hand before she answered, "He's Jake Hargrove, Lizzie.
Teddy's uncle."

Mother and Papa drove me to meet the county prosecu-
tor after lunch. His name was Walter Speaks. He had
grown up in Granby so everyone called him Wally. His
office was in Neosho, the county seat, but he had come
to visit his mother and feast on her French apple pie.

He received us in the parlor and his mother served us
iced tea before she disappeared into the dark rooms of
their old home.

Wally sat down in a chair directly across from me and
nearly rubbed his knees against mine as he asked,
"Lizzie, are you absolutely certain you saw the accused,
Jake Hargrove, shoot another man?"

With the same intensity of voice he had used, I
answered, "I am most certain."

"Then tell me the whole story, and don't leave out a
detail," Wally said as he sat back. "Not a detail. Start
with the day of the murder."

I glanced at Mother before I said, "It will have to go

back further than that. I'll have to start with the day Papa took us all on his business trip to Joplin."

Wally nodded and poised his pencil above a thick yellow pad.

So I told all. Starting with Dixie Crane and the cigarette. The loft fire and Slap Happy. The hurdy-gurdy and the Lucie woman. The murder. Uncle Ben's Remedy. The wagon ride. The trip to the river. And all about the red-eyed man, Jake. They were all things I had confessed to God, and I had thought he would allow me to keep them just between him and me. I was wrong.

I sat between Mother and Papa in the buggy on the ride home. It was an experience something like being poised in the pocket of a slingshot.

If the next morning had only been laced with sunshine, I think things would have gone a lot better. But it was as dark as the cellar when I got out of bed, and the only natural light came from the bolts of lightning that seemed to be searing the tops of the pines beyond the barn.

When I went downstairs for breakfast, Mother was flitting about the table, pouring milk. She was speaking to Papa in her most perturbed tone. "Why today? Why today of all days? It's going to rain all day. There will be mud. And *muddy* bootprints all over the house."

My brothers were eating breakfast in obedient silence. Even George.

"They waited a day to connect the Thompsons," Mother argued.

"Allie Thompson's mother had died," Papa reminded.

"Well, my carpets will die if every old boot on every old foot of every old electric company man tramps through my parlor."

"We are scheduled for today. And today it shall be," Papa said firmly as he stood up to leave.

Jack went to the door with Papa and helped him slip into his rain slicker before he stormed off the porch. Then Jack gathered Edman and George and they set out to do the chores.

Mother sat down at the table beside me and started to say something, but Hateful Hanna came in from the parlor and wanted Aunt Mittie to help her knot a thread in her embroidery.

Hanna gave me a look of superior contempt as she flicked her blond locks away from me.

Mother stood up, patted my arm, and pointed toward the stairs. I followed her to her bedroom and sat down in the big wing chair beside the window. Mother pulled a footstool up beside me and sat down. We watched the storm build for a while before Mother said, "I'm upset about everything I heard you tell Wally Speaks yesterday."

"I'm sorry, Mother," I said softly.

"Sometimes saying you're sorry, even truly feeling sorry, isn't enough, Lizzie. Sometimes you have to answer for your actions in a way you never imagined."

"Are you going to punish me, Mother?"

"The part of this that is between you and me, we'll settle later," Mother answered.

"Then who am I going to answer to?"

"I'm afraid you'll answer to everyone if . . . if you testify in court against Jake Hargrove."

"You want *me* to get up in front of a lot of people and tell everything that happened?"

"I want you to do what you think is right."

"Mother, he's a murderer. He killed one man and tried to kill me. Don't you believe me?"

"I do believe you, Lizzie, I do. But Wally says there is barely enough evidence to even keep Jake Hargrove locked up, much less enough to try him."

"What about Teddy?"

"He denies seeing anything. He says you fell asleep and dreamed it. No one from the Longman Medicine Show will even testify you left camp with Jake Hargrove. And that woman swears he was with her in Joplin until hours before the posse caught up with them."

"How long do we have?" I asked.

"Three days to gather evidence. Then the sheriff will have to let Jake Hargrove go free."

"Is Wally Speaks searching for clues?"

"He traveled by train to Kansas to interview people in the medicine show. He should be back by tomorrow morning. There's nothing we can do until then."

Mother patted my knee and went downstairs. I sat alone in her bedroom until I heard what sounded like thunder coming in the front door. I went to the top of the stairs and watched as the men from the electric company barged inside and dumped their equipment beside the parlor door. In a matter of minutes, they were busy drilling holes in the wall, running line through them, and making a total mess of Mother's nice tidy house.

After supper the clouds drifted eastward and the sun seesawed on top of the hill beyond the lane leading to the farm. I sat in the front porch swing, watching the sun set and wondering what I would do if Jake were let out of jail. I was seriously afraid he might come after me and shut up the tattletale once and for all.

Hanna brought me a cup of tea and sat down in the rocker beside the swing. I only nodded a thank you and wondered what she was up to.

"It would be very silly for you to take Mr. Hargrove to court," she finally offered sweetly.

"Why is that, Cousin Hanna?"

"Because you could be mistaken. And, besides, that old peddler probably had it coming. Some folks say he stole —"

"Hanna, 'that old peddler' was a man. A living, breathing man. Jake Hargrove murdered him."

"Teddy says he didn't —"

I dropped my teacup and caught Hanna by her arm. "You've talked to Teddy? Papa said he left town to visit relatives after he was questioned by the sheriff."

"Maybe I have," she answered coyly.

"And he told you his uncle didn't shoot that man?"

Hanna pulled her arm away and said, "That's right. And now you're in trouble for the hundredth time this summer because you broke the teacup."

I looked down. The cup was cracked and bleeding tea all over the porch. I stood up and bashed the cup with the heel of my shoe. "How's that, Hanna? Now you can run inside and tell if you want. I've just about had it with you and your big mouth."

Hanna squealed like a pig as she stood up and ran inside. When Mother didn't come out to scold me, I figured Hanna had just retreated to her bedroom to recover from the antics of her savage cousin.

I was in bed, asleep, when I felt a nudge against my shoulder. I didn't dare roll over to see who it was. Jake had probably escaped and had searched through the bedrooms until he found me. I could almost feel a knife against my throat.

"Lizzie, it's Jack," said a voice in the dark.

I rolled toward him. "What do you want?"

"Get dressed," he ordered. "Hanna was right. Teddy didn't leave town. I know where he is."

When we were on the porch, Jack helped me pull on my shoes. "Teddy is down at the smelter."

"All right," I said as I stepped into the yard and walked across the sidewalk. I turned back to see that Jack was still on the porch. "Well, come on, I don't want to get caught doing this."

Jack whispered, "I'm not going."

I hurried back to him. "Why not?"

"This is your problem, Lizzie. About time you handled it yourself," he informed me with his brother-knows-best voice.

"Jack, if this has something to do with our bet, I concede. I was wrong. I do need you and Papa. I know I wouldn't be alive today if you both hadn't helped me. You win."

"You and I were both wrong, Lizzie. You've learned

everyone needs help sometimes. I've learned all of us need freedom to try things out on our own, whether God made us men . . . or women. It's only fair for you to be treated as an equal. It's only fair you have the responsibilities of an equal," he said firmly.

"All right, if that's what you have decided. I don't have time to argue with you now," I said as I turned back toward the road that led to the smelter. The long, dark road that led to the absolutely scariest place on earth.

Giant horned owls were calling in the trees along the lane that led from the main road to the smelter. And the wind began to blow cool and brisk, lifting the boughs of the pines and making them look like flapping wings.

As I stepped onto the porch of the smelter a coyote called shrilly from the timber and a hawk screamed a reply. The boards creaked loudly and from inside the belly of the mine I could hear rats squeaking and clawing at the walls.

I almost turned around and ran home, but what Jack had said sank in. Of course, I had to see Teddy alone. It was my responsibility. Something between Teddy and me.

I followed the maze of tunnels through the front of the mine until I stood in the main room of the smelter. It was warm there because the belly of the beast never cooled. Beside the fire, I saw a cot. On the cot was Teddy, asleep, his blond hair lying limp across his brow. He looked as if he were three years old.

I prodded him gently. "Teddy, wake up. It's Lizzie."

Teddy mumbled and rolled to his side. Then he sat

straight up, as if he had seen a ghost. "What are you doing here? My stars, I'm in my drawers!"

"I came to talk to you."

Teddy sighed and pulled his blanket over himself. "I don't have anything to say."

"All right," I offered. "You don't have to say a word."

He rubbed the sleep out of his eyes and looked at me.

"I just wanted to let you know that I understand why you can't testify against your uncle. Family is family. If Aunt Mittie or Aunt Esther had done something bad, I'm not sure I wouldn't do exactly as you are doing. I know you're not afraid of your uncle. I know you have decided not to tell the truth because you love him. I respect you for that, Teddy. And I don't want there to be any hard feelings between us."

"But you are going to take my uncle to court?"

"If it's possible, yes," I said as I turned to walk away. Then I saw it, there on a crate by the door. The beaded purse Hanna had blackmailed out of me. I picked it up and held it toward Teddy. "Hanna must have left this. I'll take it to her."

Teddy didn't answer. He just sat upright in his bed with his mouth gaping open until I left.

I had wanted to choke Teddy until his eyes popped out like a frog's. I had wanted to tip over his cot and bend his arms behind his back until he yelled, "Uncle." But I couldn't. Not even with evidence in my hand that he had been seeing Hanna behind my back. I liked Teddy too much for any of that. I decided I would pay the price for friendship despite the cost.

Ahead of me along the trail a bush moved in the darkness. As it swayed from side to side as if a bull elephant was charging through it, I stopped abruptly. It wasn't an elephant at all that came to stand, straddle-legged, in the road. It was Jack. He asked huskily, "Did you see him?"

"Yes," I answered softly.

"Any good come of it?" he asked as he walked to me.

I laid my head on Jack's shoulder and felt him slip his arms around me. Weakly I said, "I got my purse back."

Jack looked down at me, questions in his eyes.

"Never mind," I told him as I let him walk me home.

❋ The Trial ❋

Mother, Papa, and I rode the freight train to Neosho the next morning because there wouldn't be a passenger train until late afternoon. We were to meet Wally Speaks to see if he'd had any luck talking to the people at the medicine show. I was also supposed to go to the county jail and officially identify Jake Hargrove as the man I was accusing of murder and attempted murder.

Mother and I had packed an overnight bag in case Wally was able to gather enough evidence to ensure that Jake Hargrove would stand trial. If he were formally accused, Jake's trial would be in only a couple of days, when the traveling judge stopped in Newton County.

Papa rented a horse and buggy at the depot and drove us to the courthouse. Wally was waiting for us on the front steps. "Good news. Well, you could even call it great news," he called out as we approached him.

"You have a witness to the murder?" Papa asked.

Wally scratched his head. "Well, it's not that great. We do have a witness from the medicine show who will testify that Jake Hargrove did take Lizzie back to Granby."

"Thought you said the circus people were staying close-mouthed about the whole affair," Papa said.

"That's how it seemed, with Mr. Longman basically threatening anyone who talked with loss of their job," Wally said.

"Who came forward?" Mother asked.

I didn't need to hear Wally answer, "Ethel Pearl Dade."

"Baby Ethel," I whispered.

Mother squeezed my shoulder and said, "Ethel is truly your friend, Elizabeth."

"Truly my friend," I repeated. And by now I knew true friends were hard to come by.

Wally took us directly to the jail. I had never been inside a place like that. It had small hallways and smelled of kerosene and disinfectant. Sheriff Benson led us into a windowless room and told me to stand on a chair and peek through a hole in the wall to identify Jake Hargrove.

I did as I was told and put my eye to the hole. Sitting in a cell away from the wall was the red-eyed man, Jake. He was drinking out of a tin cup. For some reason he looked my way and I nearly fell off the chair jerking away.

"Well, Lizzie, is that the man?" Sheriff Benson asked.

"The man with the cup, that's him," I answered.

While Papa talked with the sheriff I continued to stare through the hole. I caught a flash of tan in the corner cell and heard the distinct call of a wood thrush.

"Who's back in the cell beside Hargrove?" I asked quickly.

Sheriff Benson answered, "An old tramp."

"Slap Happy?"

"Yes, missy. That's him."

"Why is he in jail?" I begged.

The sheriff stepped toward me. "Why, you should know. You folks had me put out a warrant when he nearly burned down your barn."

"Papa," I moaned.

Papa cleared his throat. "Sheriff, that was all a misunderstanding. With this murder incident and all, we just forgot about it. Slap Happy didn't set the fire. Turns out he helped keep our barn from being a total loss."

The sheriff stroked his chin. "Funny thing about it, that old fool turned himself in. Mumbling something about the Bingmans and committing a crime. We never could make out everything he said. You know when he gets excited, he starts making those animal noises. Hard to imagine he was once a prominent businessman here in Neosho. After his wife and daughter drowned, he just went mad. Folks say he goes down to the creek near every evening and calls out for his missus and little Janie."

"Janie!" I nearly screamed. "J.E. Janie. They sound alike, right?"

Mother said, "What is it, Lizzie?"

"Remember, I said someone was calling and Hargrove looked toward the woods and that allowed me to get away. Maybe it was Slap Happy at the arbor the night of the murder."

Wally said, "It's worth a try." He turned to the sheriff and asked, "Mind if I question him?"

"May I come with you?" I asked. When Mother or Papa didn't say no, I followed Wally to Slap Happy's cell, being careful not to look at Jake.

Once inside, Slap Happy threw his arms around me. "You're all right," he said plainly. "Thought maybe you were . . ." He began to trill like a raccoon.

"Why did you come to see the sheriff?" I asked.

"Thought that man caused you some harm," Slap Happy said, pointing to Jake Hargrove. "After you saw what you saw. Wasn't that awful?"

Wally asked, "What was awful?"

Slap Happy jerked his head back and yowled before he answered, "The murder. That man over there shot that peddler fellow. I saw it all from the tree. He nearly killed this little girl, too. Terrible thing to lose a little girl. I know. From the bottom of my heart, I know."

"Would you say all that in a courtroom?" Wally asked Slap Happy.

"Don't much like crowds," Slap Happy said.

I reached out and held Slap Happy's hand. "Without your testimony, that man will probably go free."

"Then I'll talk," he said proudly. "But can I go home first? I need to check by the creek. See if Janie came back."

"The trial will be the day after tomorrow. Can you remember to be here?" Wally asked.

"Be here when the sun rises," Slap Happy said.

"Then I'll get you out," Wally promised as we left.

Before we slipped behind the iron door that separated the cells from the sheriff's office, Jake Hargrove called out to me, "You don't stand a chance, missy. I'm going to walk free tomorrow. And I'll be in every shadow for the rest of your life."

"Ignore his threats, Lizzie," Wally said as he escorted me back to Mother and Papa.

I tried, but I couldn't keep my knees from shaking like a bowl of jelly.

Papa reserved three rooms at the Fleischer Hotel. After a lunch in the hotel dining room, he returned home on the passenger train to see to the chores and bring the rest of the family back to Neosho for the trial.

It was fortunate he found us a place to stay before Jake Hargrove was formally accused. After the local newspapers announced there would be a murder trial and after the local gossips had spread the news faster than print ever could, all the hotels were booked with reporters and adventure seekers.

From what we heard through the grapevine, the first encounter Jake Hargrove had with the judge was a stormy one. Apparently, Hargrove was shocked out of his trousers that there was a witness besides a scared little girl and his mute nephew. He had socked one deputy in the nose and, we heard, it took three other men to hold him until they could put handcuffs on to get him back to his cell.

That evening, a reporter interrupted Mother and me while we were having supper and demanded to be told my side of the story. Mother poured her coffee in his lap when he wouldn't take no for an answer. The story the next day said that Mother had hit him over the head with a coffee pot. We knew from then on that fame had its price.

On August 31, court convened at ten o'clock in the morning. I was tired when I got there. The bed at the hotel had rocks in the mattress, from the way it felt. And I was so nervous when I dressed that Mother had to button my blouse for me.

The courtroom was stuffy and smelled like glue. It was crammed to the ceiling with spectators. Half of Neosho was there from what I could see, and every family in Granby was represented by an overalled farmer or a stuffed-shirt businessman.

Jake Hargrove's lawyer was a man called Hiram Parker from Kansas City. Parker was a slick-looking fellow with a sly expression. He was dressed in a gray-striped suit with a light blue shirt and shiny black shoes that made a click-click sound when he pitter-pattered across the front of the courtroom. Talk had it, he only represented people who would make the front pages of the newspapers. From the way he kept rubbing his hands over his hair to keep it slicked down, I could tell he loved the show.

When all the people had settled onto the hard benches, the judge, Ira Thompson, called the court to order by pounding a gavel on the podium he was perched behind.

Both lawyers shuffled papers at their tables and then stood up to approach the bench.

After they had said a few words in private to the judge, Hargrove's lawyer sat down and Wally directed a speech toward the jurors.

"Esteemed jury, friends, and neighbors, we are here today to listen to evidence that will prove to one and all, beyond a shadow of a doubt, that Jake Hargrove did, indeed, murder the peddler Helliot Jones in the grape arbor at Granby. I will also offer evidence that will show you how this man intended to cover up his crime by kidnapping and murdering an innocent young girl, Elizabeth Bingman."

As Wally opened his mouth to say more, a reporter from the *Granby Gazette* dragged a large camera along the side of the courtroom and steadied it on its tripod.

Judge Thompson looked suspiciously at the camera and then made a signal to the reporter to hurry up and get settled. The reporter nodded respectfully.

Again, Wally started to speak. As a single word came out, the flash bar on the camera exploded. It looked like the Fourth of July all over again. Several women screamed and fought their way into the aisle, obviously certain the whole courthouse was going up in blazes.

As the women's husbands reassured them all hell had not broken loose, and as Judge Thompson motioned for a deputy to escort the sheepish reporter out of the courtroom, Wally shrugged and said to no one in particular, "Guess that's all I have for an opening speech. Let's get on with it."

Hiram Parker, Hargrove's lawyer, rose slowly from his chair. He leaned over the table in front of him, looking at the jury and shaking his head as if he was scolding them. Then he stood up straight and "clicked" his way across the courtroom floor, pulling on the gray suspenders partially concealed by his jacket.

"We have a difference of opinion here," Parker said to the jury. "I believe I can prove Jake Hargrove was nowhere near Granby the day Helliot Jones was murdered. Indeed, I believe the people of this good county have the wrong man in custody."

"The 'people of this good county' are not on trial," Judge Thompson said firmly.

"Of course not," Parker said, with a lilt to his voice. "I know the jury will be perfectly fair." He sat down after patting Jake Hargrove on his shoulder.

Judge Thompson said, "Mr. Speaks, call your first witness."

Wally stood up and said, "Would Ethel Pearl Dade please take the stand."

Baby Ethel tottered from her seat in the back of the courtroom to the witness stand. She raised her pudgy hand to swear on the Bible. I couldn't help but feel sorry for her because most of the people in the room made little gasping sounds at the way she looked. The whispers ran through the crowd like a tide. People said things like, "Poor dear, wonder how she carries that weight?" or "Isn't she a pitiful thing?" Ethel didn't look well. Her face was blotched, and she seemed weak as she sat down after the swearing-in. They had to bring a second straight-backed chair to hold her weight.

"Do you know the defendant, Jake Hargrove?" Wally asked Baby Ethel.

"Yes, sir," she answered. "He's the poster man with the Longman shows."

"What is a poster man?"

Baby Ethel shifted in her seat and answered, "A poster man goes ahead of the circus and sees to it the shows are advertised."

"How long has Jake Hargrove been the Longman shows' poster man?"

"A year," she answered, flashing a look at Jake.

"And has Jake Hargrove been a 'good' poster man?"

Hargrove's lawyer jumped to his feet. "I object. What exactly is a 'good' poster man? And who is this young woman to judge whether or not Mr. Hargrove did, indeed, do his job well?"

Judge Thompson looked at Wally. "Mr. Speaks, make your questions more direct."

"Yes, Judge. Let's try that question another way, Ethel. Has Jake Hargrove ever been in trouble with the law?"

"I object," Parker roared.

"Be quiet," said Judge Thompson.

Ethel said, "He's been arrested a few times, mostly for being drunk in public." She bowed her head as if she had told a family secret.

"Did you ever talk about Jake Hargrove with Elizabeth Bingman?"

Ethel raised her head and said, "Yes, Lizzie and I talked about a man, who turned out to be Jake Hargrove, when she came to my tent."

Wally nodded for Ethel to continue.

She said, "Lizzie told me she saw a man murdered while she was hiding in the grape arbor with Teddy Hargrove. She didn't know who the man that killed him was, but she thought she could identify him if she saw him again."

Wally asked, "Did she see him again?"

"I believe she knew who Jake Hargrove was when he led her away from the medicine show after she had fallen asleep and ridden with us out of town."

"How do you know that?"

"She called back to me something about her 'sisters.' I thought it was unusual because she only has brothers."

"So Lizzie told you about the murder. Told you she could identify the murderer. And you did see Jake Hargrove lead Lizzie away from the medicine show," Wally summarized.

"That's correct."

Wally said, "I'm finished."

Baby Ethel started to get up, but Parker went clicking up to the judge and said, "I have a few questions, Your Honor."

It was easy to see that Baby Ethel was afraid of Hargrove's lawyer. She pulled away from him as he approached her.

Judge Thompson said, "Relax, miss. Simply tell the truth."

Baby Ethel nodded and took a deep breath.

Parker leaned against the witness stand and looked out over the people in the courtroom. "Ethel, what kind of a young lady is Elizabeth Bingman?"

"I protest!" Wally said loudly. "This is not the trial of Elizabeth Bingman."

"But Your Honor," Parker pleaded, "that girl is the key witness, and I was merely trying to establish —"

"Sustained," the judge mumbled, turning his attention back to Baby Ethel.

Parker sighed. "All right, Ethel, you said you talked to Elizabeth Bingman about the *murder*."

"That's right," Ethel said.

"What day was that?"

"The day after it happened."

"Did Elizabeth come by to see you often while you were in town, or was this a one-time visit?"

Ethel smiled. "Lizzie visits me a lot when we're in Granby. She stops by nearly every day."

"Did you see Elizabeth the day of the alleged murder?"

"Yes," Ethel said slowly, "she came by."

"Would you tell us, Miss Dade, how Elizabeth Bingman was dressed when she came to visit you, and who she was with?"

Baby Ethel looked down and mumbled, "Lizzie was with Teddy Hargrove, and she was dressed like a . . . boy."

There were some whispers in the crowd. I especially heard old Mrs. Pierson from the boarding house warming up her chops. Aunt Mittie always said that that woman's tongue wagged from both ends.

"And, Miss Dade," Parker continued, "what do you suppose Elizabeth Bingman was doing dressed like a boy?"

"Why don't you ask Lizzie?" Baby Ethel blurted.

Parker smiled at Baby Ethel and then at the judge, turning to cast his malicious grin at the jury and crowd. "I intend to ask her. I intend to. But for now, let's go back to the afternoon after the alleged murder, Miss Dade. You said Elizabeth Bingman came to your tent and *told* you about the murder?"

"Yes, sir," Baby Ethel answered wearily.

"But you didn't actually *see* a murder?"

"No, sir."

"And you say Jake Hargrove did lead Elizabeth Bingman away from the medicine show, but you didn't *see* anything but them riding away together?"

"No, sir. Except for what Lizzie said —"

"That will be all, Your Honor," Parker said quickly.

Baby Ethel walked past me on her way to the back of the courtroom. I reached over and touched her hand. She smiled sweetly and hurried on by.

"Call your next witness, Mr. Speaks," Judge Thompson said.

Wally stood up and called a deputy to him. They whispered back and forth for a little while before the deputy left the courtroom and returned with Slap Happy.

Slap Happy had been staying at the stables until it was his turn to testify. When he walked up the aisle to the witness stand, he had hay all over him and the missing Santee on his shoulder.

The bird cawed, "Santee's a bad boy, bad boy!"

Aunt Mittie stood up and scolded, "I'll say you're a bad one. You get right over here." She held out her hand, and the myna flew to his mistress. Aunt Mittie gave Slap Happy an annoyed look as she sat down with Santee resting on her arm.

Wally led Slap Happy to the witness stand and swore him in. After Slap Happy had promised to tell the truth, he looked up at the judge and said, "Been a long time since I've seen you, Ira."

The judge nodded knowingly.

Slap Happy laughed and said, "Why, when we were boys we almost ended up in front of a judge a few times. Now there you are sitting on that throne making the decisions. I'm right proud of you, Ira."

Parker stood up and said loudly, "Can we get on with it?" He pulled a watch out of his pocket and glanced at the time.

Judge Thompson ignored Parker and said, "I'm pleased to see you again, Hap. Now if you'll sit down, we can proceed."

Slap Happy nodded and sat down.

Wally asked, "Mr. Hap, where were you the evening of the murder?"

"I saw it all from a tree," Slap Happy chattered.

The crowd laughed.

"What were you doing in a tree?" Wally asked hesitantly.

"Sitting."

"Sitting?"

"Real still. Sitting and listening."

"Listening for what?"

"Listening to hear if my little girl, Janie, had come home," Slap Happy explained carefully.

There was more murmuring in the crowd.

Wally continued, "What did you see happen at the arbor?"

Slap Happy pointed to Jake Hargrove. "I saw that man shoot and kill the old peddler." He turned and pointed to me. "Then he grabbed that little girl and held her with a gun at her throat."

"And what did you do about all this?"

"I called out and the man let the girl go after she kicked him good," Slap Happy said. He turned to Judge Thompson and smiled.

"No further questions, Your Honor," Wally said as he went back to his seat.

Parker came toward Slap Happy as if he were a wolf stalking a rabbit. Slap Happy sat forward and stared into the lawyer's eyes.

"You were in a tree when you saw the alleged murder?" Parker asked.

"A *real* murder," Slap Happy said.

Parker repeated, "You were in a tree?"

Slap Happy nodded that he was.

"Now tell us again what you were doing in that tree."

"I live in the trees," Slap Happy answered with an offended tone.

"With the birds?" Parker asked coyly.

With great pride Slap Happy added, "And with the squirrels." Then he let out a long series of ticking sounds that should have called every rodent in Newton County.

Parker stepped back at the vocal display and turned toward the jury with a surprised expression. When he again stood in front of Slap Happy, he said, "You certainly have a great talent, Mr. Hap. Being able to mimic all those animal noises. Maybe you should try to get a job with the circus."

Slap Happy answered with alarm, "Don't much like

crowds." Then he surveyed the courtroom with great seriousness and began to tremble.

"Something wrong, Mr. Hap?" Parker asked with mock concern.

"I need to go," Slap Happy answered.

"But the trial isn't over."

"Need to go."

Parker started to say something more, but Slap Happy turned to Judge Thompson and said, "Ira, I really need to go."

Over Parker's complaints, Judge Thompson said, "Hap, I appreciate you coming in and talking to us. You may leave now. If we need you, we'll find you."

Jake Hargrove stood up and yelled, "You're not going to take his testimony as the truth, are you, Judge?"

Just then, Santee flew from Aunt Mittie's hand to Hargrove's shoulder. He piped, "Bad boy! Bad, bad, bad boy! Bang! Bang!"

Hargrove began to swat at the bird, cursing and calling everyone liars. He yelled at his lawyer, "Thought you said this was an open-and-shut case? Thought you said they didn't have as much of a chance as a block of ice in hell? Now they're all listening to a lying fatty, a loony old tramp, and a feathered tongue! You call this a trial!"

Judge Thompson pounded the podium with his hammer and shouted, "Come to order!" as the crowd began to cheer both for Hargrove and against him.

Parker pulled Hargrove down to his seat and Judge Thompson said, "Mr. Hargrove, you and your lawyer will have the opportunity to present your side of the story."

Hargrove pounded both his fists on the table.

Wally took a tiny step toward the judge.

"Mr. Speaks, do you have anyone left to call?" Judge Thompson asked.

Wally said, "I intend to ask Elizabeth Bingman to the stand."

There was an excited murmur in the crowd.

Judge Thompson wiped his brow with the back of his hand. "I've had too much excitement for one day. I'm getting on in years, you know. We will recess until tomorrow morning. Then the state may call its last witness, and, Mr. Parker, you may have the opportunity to dazzle all us poor country folk with your city ways after that."

We rose for the judge to leave, then stepped back out of the reporters' way as they ran out the door to write their stories.

One reporter caught Aunt Mittie as we were getting into the buggy and asked her about Santee.

Aunt Mittie said, "I don't know about the other witnesses. They are human and prone to make mistakes, but I can tell you one thing, this bird has never told a lie in his life." With that said she regally escorted the myna into the buggy.

The reporter from the *Granby Gazette* took a picture of Santee as we rode toward the hotel. The bird was on the front page of every newspaper in Missouri the next day above the caption "MYNA BIRD TURNS STOOL PIGEON!"

❋ The Verdict ❋

When my brothers and I were little kids, Papa would take us nearly every week in the summer to the icehouse. He would let us play, barefoot, on the huge hunks of ice that were buried in sawdust to keep from melting. We always got very cold feet and sawdust in our throats. The day I was to testify at the trial I felt the exact same way.

I had so many butterflies in my stomach I didn't have room for any breakfast, so I went into the courtroom with a growling belly.

After all the initial formalities, Wally called me to the witness stand. I placed my hand on the Bible and began to quote scripture to myself, "The Lord is my Shepherd, I shall not want, he leadeth me inside the stuffy courtroom . . ."

Wally helped me be seated and asked me to state my name.

I said, "Elizabeth Lee Bingman." I sounded as if I had a bucket over my head.

"Tell us what you saw at the grape arbor the evening of the murder," Wally said.

"Teddy and I saw that man" — I pointed to Jake Hargrove — "kill another man."

"Did the defendant know you saw him commit the crime?" Wally asked.

Parker yelled, "I object!"

Judge Thompson said, "Overruled. Continue."

"He knew I saw him and he caught me as I tried to go home."

"What about your friend Teddy?"

"Teddy got away. I thought he ran for help."

"Was that what Teddy did?"

"No. I didn't see Teddy again until a couple of days ago. Someone seemed to call to Jake Hargrove from the woods and when he turned to listen, I kicked him and got away. My brother Jack found me in the timber next to our farm and took me home."

"When did you see Jake Hargrove again?"

"He was sent by the medicine show people to take me back to Granby after I accidently went to sleep in the back of one of their show wagons."

"What happened on the trail?"

"Jake Hargrove made plans to murder me."

Several people gasped.

"How do you know that?" Wally asked.

I breathed deeply and glanced at Jake. "He all but told me."

"How did he intend to kill you?"

"He planned to shoot me."

Wally questioned, "Why didn't he?"

"His girlfriend, Dixie Crane, joined us on the trail and asked him not to shoot me."

"Why?"

"She said he didn't need two murders on his head. That he should just push me into the river and hope that I'd drown."

"Did he push you in the river?"

"He hit me on the head and knocked me into Shoal Creek. I was able to swim to shore. I am beholden to Miss Crane for my life."

Wally said, "That's all."

Mr. Parker cleared his throat as he stood up. He stared at me for a long moment before he walked toward the witness stand. "You know what, Miss Bingman?" he asked.

"What?"

"I'm surprised Mr. Speaks didn't ask you to go on in detail about this supposed murder you saw in the grape arbor."

I shifted toward him. "Why is that?"

"You seem so capable of spinning tales. This crowd would love to hear the story in detail," Parker said slyly.

"I object," Wally said.

"Keep your questions to the point, Mr. Parker," Judge Thompson said flatly.

Parker nodded and said, "Miss Bingman." His voice echoed in my ears as if he was talking to me from inside a well. When I looked at him, it appeared he had a twin beside him. Finally, I managed to focus on the handkerchief in his coat pocket. It was wadded up as if it had been used.

"Miss Bingman," he called again, "where were you the evening of the alleged murder that made it possible for you to see such a 'horrendous' crime as Jake Hargrove has been accused of?"

"At the grape arbor, sir," I answered weakly.

"Where is that, missy?"

"At the edge of Granby."

"Do you go there often?" he asked nastily.

"No, sir."

"What were you doing there that afternoon?"

I glanced toward the back of the courtroom. Teddy walked in with his mother and sat down a couple of rows behind his uncle Jake where two chairs had been marked "reserved."

"I was hiding there, sir," I answered as I continued to stare at Teddy. Finally, he looked at me and pulled at his collar.

"Hiding from whom?" he asked dramatically.

"Hiding from my brothers, Jack and Edman." I saw both of them slide down in their seats.

"Why?"

"Because I was afraid they were going to whip the socks off Teddy and make me watch," I answered hatefully. "What in the world does all this have to do with Jake Hargrove shooting a man to death?"

Judge Thompson pounded his gavel on the podium and said sternly, "Miss Bingman, that is enough."

"Yes, sir," I said, almost crying. I knew my face was as red as a ripe tomato.

The prodding lawyer continued. "What were you doing, or what had you done, to make your brothers angry with you?"

I sat up and directed a steely gaze at the smart-mouthed lawyer. "Teddy and I attended the hurdy-gurdy show. That's what I was doing in boy's clothing. His uncle Jake got the tickets for us."

"A hurdy-gurdy show?" the lawyer whined. "What *is* a hurdy-gurdy show?"

I didn't answer.

The judge reminded me, "You have been asked a question, Miss Bingman."

I drew a quick breath. "You know what they are. There's music, a little crank organ or something. And a show. Last year they had acrobats."

Parker leaned toward me. "We aren't talking about last year, Miss Bingman. Tell us about the show *this* year. Did you see *acrobats?*"

"Acrobats aren't as popular as they used to be," I started.

Judge Thompson drummed his fingers on the podium. "Answer the question, miss."

"All right. All right," I said. "*This* hurdy-gurdy show was women dancing around on the stage in their underwear, and the crowd of men who paid to see them applauded and cheered as if they had never seen filled drawers before."

The men in the courtroom laughed, and some old woman said loudly, "My word, my word!"

Parker didn't seem to be influenced by the audience's response to my humor, but instead paced and came to stand directly in front of me. He leaned toward me and asked softly, "Should a young *lady* spend her time at a hurdy-gurdy show?"

"No, sir," I admitted. Then I quickly balanced the scales of equality in my mind and added, "A young *man* shouldn't spend his time at a hurdy-gurdy either."

Parker smiled and walked to his table. He pulled out a paper and read it to himself. Then he asked me, "You mentioned seeing Jake Hargrove's girlfriend on the trail."

"Yes, sir. Dixie Crane," I answered. I saw Dixie sitting directly behind Jake. She was wearing a pale blue dress and her hair was braided tightly over her ears. She looked as if she had just finished teaching Sunday School.

"Was that the first time you met Miss Crane?" Parker asked as he again walked toward me.

"I met Miss Crane in Joplin when my family traveled there for a holiday," I answered.

"Where in Joplin did you meet her?"

"At a bar."

"A *bar*?" Parker said loudly.

"I met her there when my brother and I were invited in for a *root beer*."

"And a cigarette?"

"Let's not forget the cigarette," I said flatly. "The one I nearly burned our barn down with."

Some of the crowd laughed. I glanced at Mother. She was sitting like Lot's wife in the Bible. The one who turned into a pillar of salt.

Parker glanced at the jury before he continued, "What were you and Teddy Hargrove doing at the grape arbor?"

"I told you — hiding."

"What were you doing while you were *hiding*?"

Wally jumped up like a jack rabbit and yelled, "I object! As I said before, this is not Elizabeth Bingman's trial."

"I'll answer the question," I said hotly. "I fell asleep."

"*Where* did you fall asleep while you were in the arbor?"

"On Teddy's shoulder."

"Is Teddy your boyfriend?"

I looked toward Teddy. He was sitting on the edge of his seat, staring at me. "Teddy Hargrove is my friend."

"Have you ever shown any affection toward him?"

"What do you mean?"

The lawyer smirked. "Have you ever *kissed* him?"

"One time," I answered quickly. "At my birthday party, and my brother Jack dragged him through the barn lot for it."

The people laughed and Parker sat down, apparently pleased he had made a fool out of me.

Judge Thompson leaned over his podium. "Elizabeth, it looks as if you've had a busy summer."

"Yes, sir," I agreed.

"It also seems Mr. Parker, over there, is trying his best to make you appear as a scatter-brained, impulsive child. What do you think?"

Parker roared, "I object!"

"Oh, sit down," Judge Thompson said nearly as loudly.

"Your Honor, I think I made myself look foolish. I know what's been said has made me look real bad. It's all true to some degree or another. I can't change any of that now. But, I do know one thing. While Teddy and I were sitting in the arbor, Jake Hargrove and Helliot Jones had a card game. When Mr. Jones lost the hand he stood up and cursed at Mr. Hargrove. He also pulled a knife out of his pocket. Mr. Hargrove took a revolver out of his coat and shot Mr. Jones in the chest. Then, when Mr. Jones was lying on the ground, Mr. Hargrove fired three more shots into him. He caught me and planned to kill me, too. I got away. Later that week I bought a bottle of Uncle Ben's Remedy and drank most of it. It knocked me out and I ended up riding with the medicine show to Kansas. Jake Hargrove was the man who brought me back. He tried again to kill me, but his girlfriend talked him into pushing me into the river. He did, but I survived to tell this story."

Parker stood up and said, "You say Teddy Hargrove was with you in the arbor the evening of the alleged murder?"

"Teddy was with me. I know what Teddy saw, but I respect his feelings about his own uncle, the accused. I don't hold anything against him, and do you know what, Mr. Parker?"

"What?"

"I'd gladly kiss him again."

I sat down beside Mother and waited while they swore in Dixie Crane. Mother had a sizzle about her as if she was a pan of popcorn ready to explode.

Dixie adjusted her skirt as she sat down.

Parker smiled at her and asked, "Miss Crane, how long have you known Jake Hargrove?"

"Jake and I go back a long ways," she started, then said in a more hushed tone, "I mean, we've been friends for many years."

"Where was Jake Hargrove the day of the alleged murder?"

"He was with me in Joplin. Jake always comes to visit when the medicine show is in the area." Her voice was dripping maple sugar.

"He was with you?"

"Yes. We had dinner and went . . . dancing." Dixie smiled sweetly.

It was really hard to imagine Jake Hargrove dancing. He looked as if he could mash a woman's toes.

Parker rubbed his chin. "Let me ask you a few questions about Elizabeth Bingman."

Dixie looked at me.

Parker followed her gaze across the room and smiled at me. "Let's see, Miss Crane, you did meet Miss Bingman in Joplin?"

"Yes, sir. At the Tarwater Saloon."

"And later, where?"

"On the trail back to Granby. Jake had to take her home because she had passed out in one of the wagons and rode with the troupe to Kansas."

"And this is where Jake supposedly tried to murder her?"

"That child," Dixie snorted. "That child is such a character. First time I saw her she was with her little brother, out walking the streets, looking for adventure, no doubt. I thought, She's a case. What a gift of gab. What a spellbinder."

"Do you mean Jake Hargrove didn't try to murder her?"

Dixie laughed. "Goodness, no! That child *jumped* into the river and said she would swim home. Jake had nothing to do with it. Why, he even tried to pull her out, but the current swept her downstream. Next thing we knew there was a sheriff's posse running us into Neosho for murder."

"Thank you, Miss Crane," Parker said as he sat down.

Wally got up. "My, my, my, Miss Crane. Your story seems to differ greatly from Elizabeth Bingman's."

"Girls will be girls," Dixie said as if she were a sage.

"And women will be women," Wally added. "Let's go back to the evening of the murder. You say you were with Jake Hargrove?"

"That's right," Dixie said.

"In Joplin?"

"That's right."

"How many miles from Joplin is Granby?"

"About thirty, I guess," Dixie said, looking toward Jake.

"By road?"

"By road."

"How about across fields?"

"I have no idea," Dixie said, looking scared.

"I put a rider out and had him time himself between Granby and Joplin. Took him just a little over two hours, taking all the shortcuts, you know, working at it."

"What are you getting at?" Dixie asked, with an edge to her voice.

"I'm saying it is more than possible for Jake Hargrove to have murdered Helliot Jones at the grape arbor in Granby and then hightailed it to Joplin to be with you for a round of — let's see now, what did you call it — dancing?"

"That right, Jake?" Dixie asked, looking at Hargrove.

Jake hit himself on the forehead with the palm of his hand and gave Dixie a look that said he thought she must be the stupidest person on earth.

"That's all," Wally said.

Dixie climbed down from the witness stand and walked slowly back to her seat. Her hips swayed from side to side, as if she were balancing a great load. She stopped to smile at the banker from Granby before she sat down. The banker smiled back and got his wife's elbow deposited in his side.

Parker stood up and called Teddy to the stand.

I knew Teddy would be the last witness. Wally had told us Jake would not testify on his own behalf. We suspected his lawyer didn't want to risk another display of Jake's temper.

Teddy looked real nice, wearing his white suit with a sky blue shirt. I could tell he was scared. And I watched as he avoided looking directly at his uncle. He couldn't appear to find anywhere to focus and finally ended up looking at me. I smiled at him.

Mr. Parker asked him to state his name and Teddy said, "Theodore Roosevelt Hargrove."

"Where were you the evening of the alleged murder?"

Teddy answered, "In the grape arbor at the edge of Granby with Elizabeth Bingman."

"What were you doing there?"

Teddy smiled at me. He didn't answer.

Parker flashed him a look of reprimand. "This is a serious situation, Mr. Hargrove."

Teddy sat up tall.

"Were you hiding in the arbor?" Parker asked shrilly.

Wally objected, saying, "You're leading the witness."

Judge Thompson said, "Sustained."

Parker restated his question. "What were you doing in the arbor?"

Teddy didn't say anything. He looked away from the lawyer and shook his head as if he was trying to remember.

Judge Thompson said, "Answer the question, son."

I felt a million chills run up my spine as Teddy turned toward me and said, "I was hiding from Lizzie's brothers. While we were there Helliot Jones, the peddler, played cards with my uncle Jake. After he lost, he pulled a knife and tried to get back his money. Uncle Jake shot him in self-defense, but Uncle Jake always had a terrible temper, so he filled the man with lead before he left the camp. Everything else Lizzie said about that evening is true. I don't know about the medicine show. I wasn't around for that. I was busy hiding out. Trying to avoid my responsibilities. Trying to forget about what happened. I came here today to lie for my uncle. Sorry, Uncle Jake, I just couldn't do it. You were wrong. I was wrong for agreeing with your lawyer to help you."

Parker sat down with a thump and began to put papers into his satchel.

Teddy continued, "I knew just how wrong I was when Lizzie came to me the other night and told me she understood the position I was in. But I can only say to her that I'm sorry. I hope we can still be friends, Lizzie."

I nodded that we could and above all the commotion

in the courtroom that followed Teddy's testimony, I could still hear those last words he had spoken to me.

Jake Hargrove was sentenced to fifteen years in jail for the murder of Helliot Jones and ten years for attempted murder. Dixie Crane was arrested and accused of perjury and conspiracy to commit murder. Hiram Parker was disbarred.

We found all this out from the newspaper the hotel desk clerk brought us while we were packing to go back to Granby. Papa wouldn't let any of us stay in the courtroom to hear the closing statements or the sentencing. He said our part was finished, and we had to go on with our own lives, minus the excitement.

We took the passenger train to Granby that afternoon. When we arrived at the depot, Papa got our horses, wagon, and buggy out of the livery stable and had the boys get them ready to travel home.

Aunt Mittie's beau met her to drive her home and she dragged Hanna along with her. Papa took the boys in the wagon to the smelter to see that everything was running smoothly. Mother and I took the buggy back to the farm.

When we turned up the lane to the house we could see the tangle of wires running from the electric poles along the front porch, out to the barn, and past to all the other outbuildings on the place.

"Look at that," Mother said softly as she reined the horse to a stop. "Your papa has the whole farm looking as if it were tangled in a spider's web. But, that's progress, daughter."

I could tell from her tone she wasn't finished.

"I intend to write Thomas Edison to tell him how I feel about his invention, and send him a bill for my damaged carpets," she added, laughing. "I'll bet he has a stack of them already. I do intend to make some good out of it, and with any support at all, taxes on that electricity will fund a clinic."

Mother sat quietly for a moment, then said, "I can't deny it, Lizzie. I was proud of how you were able to testify. I was proud of your conviction to see that the truth was told. Times are changing. When I was young, a girl wouldn't even have been listened to by her parents, much less given the opportunity to speak to the community. I hope I have raised you right. I hope I have given you what you need to get along when you are a woman. God knows I have tried to pass on all that I was taught."

"I love you, Mother," I said, as I leaned my head on her shoulder.

"And I love you, too, Elizabeth. But, darling daughter, I do not even vaguely like many of the things you have done this summer."

Her tone had changed, and I knew the Bible would soon be in my lap. I was certainly surprised when, after Mother had parked the buggy, she took me by the hand and led me to that place of undeserved honor in the Bingman household, the woodshed. There, beneath our first glowing electric light, Mother applied, with the help of her riding quirt, a fair dose of equality to the seat of my bloomers.

* Epilogue *

Baby Ethel found work with another circus sideshow and became so popular she was asked to tour Europe to entertain the troops in the Great War.

Slap Happy remained in the woods until he became ill and spent his last days in a nice boarding house at the expense of Judge Ira Thompson.

Teddy and his family moved to Springfield to start a new life. He wrote me until he enlisted in the army. His mother sent me notice that Teddy died, a hero, in the Meuse-Argonne offensive in 1918.

Hanna married Jeffrey Wilson, the banker's son. They moved to Kansas City and she immediately began having babies. I only gave her my beaded purse on her wedding day. We haven't spoken since.

As for Jack, he took his speech to the state competition. The rules demanded he not change a line of it, so he had to read it word for word as he had at the Lux Theater in Granby. I could tell his views about women were changing. He delivered it with all the enthusiasm of an undertaker who had just been told the cemetery had flooded. He got a tin medal for last place. I saw him fling it under a bench when he didn't think anyone was looking.

In 1920, the year I turned twenty-one, women were allowed to vote in the presidential election. Mother and I hurried to the polls that crisp November morning, in order to be among the first to cast our ballots.

Mother voted for the Republican, Warren Harding. I voted for the Democratic standard-bearer, James M. Cox. Jack said it was typical of women to ride together to the polls only to cancel out each other's vote.

I didn't mind the criticism that came from the men in my family. Or even that Mother's candidate was certain to win. There was satisfaction enough in returning from the polls, sitting beside my mother as she steered our new Model T down the rutted main street of my hometown.

Mother never took me to the woodshed again. To make her point in a discussion, she would simply switch on an electric light. The message came to me loud and clear. Progress and equality, both lighting the world. During those growing-up years the three of us became very close: Mr. Edison, Mother, and me.